AN INSANE PLAN—
TO MEET A DESPERATE THREAT

It was a job for fools or madmen. The job was to take a world of backward peasants, develop their science, and train them to ride spaceships instead of horses, using laser guns instead of swords. Could 2500 years of normal human evolution be condensed into a single decade? Harlen, Smith, and Sorenstein weren't sure, but they were willing to try. Maybe they were fools, and maybe they were madmen—they certainly acted that way, now and then. But as Terran spies on the peasant world, they knew this was the only hope of holding off an invasion of mysterious aliens who were threatening to take over the entire galaxy!

Also by Michael Kurland

TRANSMISSION ERROR
THE UNICORN GIRL

TEN YEARS TO DOOMSDAY

Michael Kurland
and
Chester Anderson

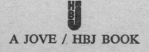

A JOVE / HBJ BOOK

First Jove/HBJ edition published December 1977

Printed in Canada

Jove/HBJ books arc published by Jove Publications, Inc. (Harcourt Brace Jovanovich), 757 Third Avenue, New York, N.Y.
10017

The authors would like to take this opportunity to dedicate their first joint opus to each other.

TEN YEARS TO DOOMSDAY

1

The *Terran Beaver*, a light cruiser of the Federation Navy, was moving slowly through the twenty-seventh day of a purely routine survey operation at the leading edge of the galactic rim. For the men on board the trip had been, as usual, a milk run. All the work the job required was performed automatically by the ship, leaving the crew of eleven free to play at being spacemen.

At 1520 Greenwich, a nameless blip appeared on the distant identification screens. D-I Screenman (Third Class) Ritch Haln idly thumbed the button that ordered the *Beaver* to start recording what she'd already been recording for three minutes. Then, quite unaware that he'd just entered history, D-I/3 Haln returned to the novel he'd been reading.

At 1545, the *Beaver* interrupted Haln by politely saying "Bleep" at him. He looked languidly up at the screens, and promptly lost his languor. The nameless blip had grown into a ship of unknown origin but clearly cruiser class. Haln played on the buttons stretched out before him like a nervous pianist, setting off a toccata of bells, alarms, and automatic processes all over the *Beaver*. He closed his performance by sounding the first General Alarm in the ship's history, and then leaned back and waited for anything to happen.

Standard identification signals were beamed at the stranger on all probable frequencies. The Captain and the staff xenologist arrived on the bridge simultaneously, both babbling. The *Terran Beaver* rocked with excitement.

This was a Contact! As its image grew in the screens, it became increasingly obvious that the stranger belonged to a completely unknown race, the first new civilization the Federation had met in more than three hundred years. Communication would be established; the newcomers would be invited to join the Federation and would, of course, accept the invitation; the crew of the *Beaver* would all become heroes and be awarded enormous bonuses, and . . .

At 1551, the stranger opened fire with an impressive battery of weapons. The *Beaver's* defenses, which had never been used before, cut in automatically; equally automatic counteroffensive measures were taken by the *Beaver's* computer, and by 1551.0685, the unidentified ship was nothing but an expanding cloud of radiant gasses, suitable only for spectroscopic analysis.

This ended the first action the Federation Navy had seen in nearly a thousand years. The *Terran Beaver* ran for home.

2

"It's a Mother-lorn bad night, I'm learning." Hurd Gar-Olnyn Saarlip lurked conscientiously in the darkest doorway he could find, talking shop with himself in careful whispers. "No purses pass, no paunchy pockets. Nobles shun this darkened street. I'll sleep more hungrily tonight than I have ever slept before."

Hurd was a poet by profession, as he'd tell himself proudly, formerly bard-in-residence to a singularly noble baron who had, unfortunately, died without issue, technically speaking, thus giving Hurd a choice between having his personal service mortgage sold, possibly to a withered crone grown fond of gladiatorial sports, or defaulting on his mortgage by running away and becoming an outlaw. To Hurd Gar-Olnyn Saarlip, poet and son of poets, this was as close to no choice at all as he cared to approach.

"Alas, the night is cold," he reminded himself, "and no one passes by who is more prosperous than I am. Mother, grant this one request: a merchant thick with wine and wealth—or even a barkeep's apprentice toting home the night's receipts. Though," after a pause, "apprentices are often rowdy and unwilling to be robbed." He shivered.

Besides being a poet, Hurd was a footpad, cutpurse, mugger, second-story man and general duty all 'round felon, as need and opportunities arose. Though his criminal career would probably lead him to the stake and Mother's Wrath, crime was a traditional and even honorable subvocation for poets on the planet Lyff. And Hurd could always comfort himself with the knowledge that his execution, if spectacular enough, would do wonders for his reputation, create an instant demand for his poems, and vastly enrich his publishers and heirs, if any.

The gaslight at the corner flickered nervously in the winter-honed wind, casting ominous shadows against the heavy-timbered buildings that lined the narrow street. Hurd continued to shiver.

"Mother, grant your thieving but devoted child this one request, and . . ." At the sound of a tentative footstep just around the corner Hurd stopped whispering, shrank further into the dim-lit doorway, and stood silently, still trembling from the cold.

A tall, thin young man in warm and costly garments turned the corner and paused uncertainly. He seemed to be hunting for a street sign or landmark. Finding none, he moved slowly down the street toward Hurd's hiding place. "Your worthless offspring blesses you," Hurd subvocalized, in case Mother was listening.

The stranger was obviously lost. Furthermore, the cut and quality of his heavy clothes and the comfortable roundness of his purse proclaimed the stranger wealthy. Since he was both wealthy and clean-shaven at a time when all the rich men in Lyffdarg were sporting beards, the stranger was most likely a foreigner, possibly a merchant from the western seaport town of Freydarg, and would not be missed, should Hurd be forced to deal harshly with him. And best of all, the stranger was walking with a heavy, slow, unsteady gait that might well mean he was drunk and relatively helpless. Hurd forgot the cold.

When he passed Hurd's doorway, the stranger was peering intently at a building across the street. Hurd thanked Mother silently for this blessing.

The narrow street meandered like a stream, thanks to Lyffdarg's having been laid out by grazing cattle. As the stranger moved on toward the unlighted swerve, Hurd slipped out of the doorway and followed him.

Hurd's knife was in his hand—strictly for use in threatening the stranger, he reminded himself queasily, thinking of the elaborate punishments reserved for murderers of wealthy men—and there was no metal in his purse to jingle and betray him, so he was able to maintain a useful silence easily. Good. Even a very drunken stranger, and especially a young one, might become unmanageable if prematurely alarmed.

The stranger turned the corner and walked into the darkness. Hurd gave him time to get well out of sight, and then followed him.

The stranger was silhouetted against a distant grog-shop lantern, and Hurd was invisible, a darkness in darkness. This was the time. One chop with the blade of the hand against the stranger's nape, one stunning blow, and Hurd would eat fine meat and drink delicate wines for a month.

Hurd leaped.

And rolled down the glistening wet cobblestones ahead of the stranger like an ill-packed sack of grain.

From where he lay among the cobbles, Hurd had a fine view of the sole of the stranger's boot descending on his neck. This was far from reassuring.

"Oh please, Your Worship, spare me," Hurd cringed. "I'm just a poor man, driven to this sad extreme by hunger and the weak cries of my children, and I've never done a thing like this before." Then, realizing that he was in the position he'd planned for the stranger, and that there was no way he could account for this dismaying reversal of roles, he broke rhythm to ask, "What happened?"

The stranger was unperturbed. "Lever and fulcrum," he said calmly. "Elementary physics, that's all. Could you please direct me to the home of Tarn Gar-Terrayen Jellfte, Physician to the King, and so on?"

"Physics you call it that cast me to the ground?"

"The ancient word is 'judo,' if that helps you any, which I doubt. Where does Doctor Jellfte live?" The stranger seemed not to notice that his foot was firmly and heavily set on Hurd's skinny neck.

"Are you going to turn me over to the Guards?" Hurd was acutely aware of the stranger's foot. Indeed, it was growing heavier by the second.

"Of course not, man. I want directions, not your blood. However . . ." The stranger paused.

Hurd didn't want to learn how the stranger intended to finish that sentence. "Directions in Lyffdarg are often confusing," he babbled, "and strangers are frequently known to get lost. But the house of The Reverend Lord Surgeon Tarn Jellfte, the worthiest heir of his great father, Terra (of whom I confess that I know very little), is only a matter of seven blocks distant, and I, who know well all the streets of the city . . ." The foot became suddenly much heavier, and Hurd lost his meter. "I'll be glad to guide you there, if it please Your Worship," he said weakly.

The stranger lifted Hurd from the cobbles and, twisting the poet's right arm behind his back in an intricate manner that promised to become extremely painful upon unreasonably little provocation, said, "Lead, and I follow. And very closely, too, you'll notice."

They moved on in silence for a while. In case Mother was still listening, Hurd filled his head with unvoiced prayers for help. But, since she had played him such an unfair and thoroughly dirty trick, he had scant hope she'd hear him.

The stranger interrupted Hurd's entreaties. "Old son, do all you Lyffdarg dwellers speak in meter all the time, and if so, may the verse be blank, or is it usual to rhyme?"

"What?"

"I said—"

"No, Lord, I heard you well the first time. Could *you* be a poet, too?" Maybe Mother was on Hurd's side after all. The Guild of Bards forbade betrayals.

"Oh." The stranger sounded relieved, somehow. "Then meter isn't necessary either. Great. I was worrying about that. The educational tapes didn't say anything about poetry, and I don't think the rest of the crew could have done it. Lyffan's hard enough to speak in prose."

"Educational tapes?" The man was obviously a foreigner, yes, but where in Mother's Hidden Garden did he pick up such outlandish words?

"You wouldn't understand. Tell me, old son, do you have a name?"

Name? Hurd wondered if he dared to tell the stranger, who was apparently not a poet after all, his real name. Then again, with his arm in this dangerous position, did he dare to lie?

They were passing a narrow alley. Out of its darkness staggered an exceedingly drunk young noble. His beard was a good half an arm long, indicating that he was at least a subduke, according to current fashions.

"Clear my path, ye Mother-lorn immoral scum," the noble snarled thickly.

"What's all *this* about?" the stranger asked. Hurd tried to hurry them on, but the stranger wanted to stand still, and Hurd had no choice but to remain with him.

"Aha! They stand defiant." The drunken noble was ferociously delighted. "Garlyn, Tchornyo, come here and see the game our Mother has provided."

Two more nobles stepped into the light. All three had half-arm beards, all three were richly and colorfully dressed, all three were very young and drunk, and now all three had drawn their swords. Hurd commended his spirit to Mother.

"What do you people want?" asked the stranger.

"Sport, ye skin-faced publican," one of the newcomers answered, swaggering.

"Your yellow blood'll do for now," the other newcomer added.

The first young noble cleared his throat and announced in a clear, loud voice, "Your mother sold herself to strangers." It would have been an insult in any culture; in

15

a civilization that worshiped a mother goddess, it was an open invitation to kill or be killed.

The stranger released Hurd, whispering, "You're a dead man if you try to run away." Then he told the nobles in a matter-of-fact tone, "Strangers refused to buy your mothers." In the silence that followed, he added, "You are your mothers' accidental sons." He was obviously prepared to improvise on this theme all night long, but before he had time to state another variation, the nobles rushed him.

Hurd took what shelter he could find in a doorway— this was his night for doorways—and watched the fight with reverential fear.

One of the nobles, though which one it was hard to determine in the dim light, lunged at the stranger, razor-sharpened sword outthrust. The stranger danced easily to one side of where the blade should have pierced him, grabbed the noble's long beard and pulled enthusiastically. The beard was false. It came off in the stranger's hand. Laughing insultingly, the stranger in one neat motion tripped the bald-faced noble and thrust the artificial beard in the face of another attacker.

The fallen noble slid across the cobblestones to within an arm's length of Hurd's hiding place. In a burst of previously unsuspected class resentment, Hurd cried out, "Sweet Mother, forgive me this blasphemous joy!" and kicked the noble's head again and again. Blood began to glisten on the stones.

Meanwhile, the stranger was trapped between the two remaining nobles. Their sword points flickered about him like dangerous insects, but he seemed miraculously to be at all times exactly where the angry swords were not. However, he could attack neither swordsman without being run through by the other. In spite of the cold, there was sweat on the stranger's brow.

"You're finished now," one of the nobles sneered, "for my blade has been dipped in Mother's Milk." (Mother's Milk was a broad-spectrum poison compounded mainly of cyanide and a vegetable alkaloid similar to curare.) The other noble remained silent, and the stranger edged toward him.

Hurd noticed at this point that the man he was kicking was thoroughly dead. "Now Mother protect me," he yelled, "for no man dies The Long Death more than once." He hurled the dead man's sword like a javelin at the noble with the poisoned blade. It passed through the noble's throat and he fell to the ground, wearing a look of indignant surprise.

"Good work, old son," the stranger said calmly. The surviving noble made a desperate lunge, then turned and ran off, shouting hysterically for help. He left his sword behind him, fixed in the stranger's right shoulder.

The noble's howling faded in the distance. Hurd and the stranger stood facing each other over the two bloody bodies. Now that he had time to think clearly again, Hurd was terrified. "We're dead," he announced, his voice flat and vacant. "They'll catch us sure. Even if they have to jail half the city to do it, they'll catch us. Then they'll spend a whole month killing us, as Mother's Law demands. And we even let a witness get away."

But the stranger was more concerned with the sword in his shoulder. He pulled it out carefully, barely wincing, and the eager blood burst forth to follow it. "Come on, old son," he said between clenched teeth. "Take me to Doc Jellfte's house. *Now.*"

They went. In spite of his terror, Hurd remembered to collect the dead men's purses. "At least I'll eat well now, until they catch me."

Tarn Gar-Terrayen Jellfte, Duke of Lyff, Physician to the King and Sponsor Appointant of the Guild of Healers, was roused from his comfortable dreams at a Mother-lorn late hour by a raucous and unseemly clamor at his front door. Like most middle-aged Lyffan nobles, he tended to be rather pompous, proper, and conservative, as well as just a little bit timid. Therefore, when he opened his door and found that his callers were a richly-clad but wounded youth and a ragged fellow who was probably a criminal of some sort, his first impulse was to cry for help. When the wounded man started speaking Terran too rapidly for the doctor, who'd neither heard nor spoken the language for twelve years, to follow, his first thought was that his assignment had been terminated, and his second impulse, nobly suppressed, was to faint.

Instead he said in halting Terran, "Speak more slowly, please. It's been a long time, and I can't understand you."

The Terran and the criminal pushed their way into the vestibule and closed the front door. "Would you rather I spoke Lyffan?" asked the young man.

"Well . . . I mean . . ." Doctor Jellfte groped for words. Finally he said, in Lyffan, "After all, it *has* been a long time."

"Great. Please raise your right hand."

Confused by it all, and convinced that the criminal was casing his house (which the criminal certainly was), Doctor Jellfte raised his hand.

The young man's Lyffan was almost as rapid and hard to understand as his Terran had been. "Do you swear by whatever deity or personal ethic guides your life to uphold and defend the Constitution of The Terran Federation of Planets to the best of your ability and to comply with the laws of The Terran Federation of Planets and the Regulations of The Federation Naval Services, which are hereby incorporated herein by reference, for the duration of this commission, so help you whatever deity or personal ethic guides your life? Say, 'I do.'"

Numbly, confusedly and automatically, Doctor Jellfte said, "Uh, I do."

"Great." The young man saluted gingerly. "Sir, you are hereby transferred from inactive to active reserve status, promoted to the rank of Lower Commander, and ordered to assume command of all naval facilities on the planet Lyff. You are furthermore instructed to cooperate in every way with Special Detail L-2 for the duration of the current emergency. It's all in here." He pulled a blood-stained envelope from his jacket pocket and handed it to the bewildered doctor. "My name's John Harlen, and for God's sake do something!"

And the young Terran collapsed.

3

The *Terran Beaver* arrived at the Federation Naval Base on Luna twenty-five days before John Harlen reported to Doctor Jellfte on Lyff. The *Beaver's* log tapes were being fed into Master Control for analysis less than half an hour after the ship's arrival, and it took the computer another half-hour to correlate the *Beaver's* adventure with everything else that had happened in the past thousand years of Federation history. Master Control's conclusions were released to the newstape networks five hours before the *Beaver's* crew was released from debriefing, making Ritch Haln one of the last people in the Home System to learn that what he had experienced was the opening shot of the First Intergalactic War.

Admiral of the Navies Edvalt Bellman, on the other hand, was the first person to get this information, because Master Control reported directly to him. He forwarded most of the computer's report to Parliament, but one section, marked CONFIDENTIAL/URGENT, he made known only to three other people, at a briefing held later that afternoon.

"We have ten years," he said, pacing as strenuously as the narrow confines of his office would allow.

The three young officers he was addressing were properly confused. "Ten years? Then what's the problem?" That was Ansgar Sorenstein, the youngest of the three, who had been, until that afternoon, a little-known newstape reporter.

"The problem," Bellman said solemnly, "is that we need fifteen." He stopped behind his desk and consulted

MC's confidential report again. "Yes," he went on, "fifteen years. Do you realize that at this moment our combat strength consists of exactly eleven ships?"

After a moment of silence, Bellman continued. "We don't know who's attacking us, of course, but we know quite a lot about them. They're obviously a warlike race, for instance. They shoot first and ask questions later, if at all. That's what happened to the *Beaver*. According to Master Control, that's what's happened to twenty-four survey ships we've lost in the past five years. The *Beaver* would have been number twenty-five, but she was a warship and could take care of herself. The enemy's weapons are almost as good as ours, the *Beaver's* log tapes prove that. And the enemy has been preparing for war God alone knows how long."

Pindar Smith raised his hand. "Sir?"

"Yes?"

Smith stood up. "I should think, sir, that with all we know about the enemy, we should have no trouble in getting ready for them. After all, ten years is a long time."

John Harlen answered that one. "There's only one thing wrong, old son," he said. "They've known about us five years longer than we've known about them."

Smith sat down again as Admiral Bellman added, "That's part of the problem, yes. The other part is that they already have a wartime economy. No doubt they started building their forces the moment they discovered us. It'll take us at least two years to get started."

"The price of peace," John Harlen muttered.

They spent half an hour discussing the problem, during which Bellman did more observing than talking. He liked what he saw. Lieutenants Harlen, Smith, and Sorenstein were the pride of the Synthesist Corps, specialists in everything, and Bellman had no doubt that they could do the job he had for them, if the job could be done at all.

John Harlen, for example, was basically a poet, and a fairly successful one at that. However, he was also a trained engineer, he had a degree in mathematics, and he'd supported himself at one time as a consulting psychologist.

Ansgar Sorenstein, the journalist, was only twenty-four years old, but already he had advanced degrees in physics, music, anthropology and organic chemistry. He was working for the newstapes for, as he put it, kicks.

Pindar Smith was a businessman. Pindar Enterprises, Ltd., the firm he founded and owned, dealt in textiles, agriculture, and nonferrous metals. Smith himself was a specialist in these fields, as well as in electronics and history. His two hobbies, logically enough, were printing and science fiction, and he'd combined these for the past eleven years in *Advanced Science Fiction and Theories,* a moderately successful magazine he wrote, edited, and published under a bewildering collection of pseudonyms.

"All right, gentlemen," said Bellman, cutting into their discussion. "You seem to understand the situation fairly well. Now perhaps you'd like to know what all of this has to do with you."

"That's fairly obvious," said John Harlen. "We're all members of the Synthesist Corps, right? That may be a coincidence, or you may be planning to pull off some kind of unorthodox operation. However, Master Control doesn't fool around with coincidences, right? We've known what we're here for ever since we arrived. All we need now are the details. What sneaky trick do you have in mind, sir?"

Bellman hadn't realized that he still knew how to blush. "Master Control has a plan . . ." he began.

"An illegal plan, I suppose," Sorenstein interjected.

"It's always an illegal plan," Smith added. "I remember that job we pulled on Maury's World—you know, when we had to burgle the—"

"Gentlemen!" Bellman refused to be embarrassed by Synthesist shop talk. The three lieutenants fell silent. "Thank you, gentlemen. This assignment concerns the planet Lyff."

"I thought so," Smith whispered. "Another contact violation."

Bellman ignored Smith. "The planet Lyff is the first Federation territory the enemy is likely to strike. According to Master Control . . ."

"But sir," Sorenstein interrupted, "Lyff isn't a member of the Federation."

"It will be. May I go on?"

"Oh sure. Don't let me bother you."

"Thank you, Lieutenant Sorenstein." Bellman paused to consult the report once more. "Yes," he said. "The planet Lyff is inhabited by what we assume to be the descendents of an early colonization attempt. We have no record of how these people came to be established on Lyff, nor do they, but it must have taken them anywhere from fifteen hundred to two thousand years to reach their present cultural level, and they are the only mammals on the planet. Even in the absence of all other evidence, this can be considered conclusive."

In the unconsciously flat tone of a trained lecturer, Bellman went on to summarize the history of the Federation's dealings with Lyff. "Twelve years ago, the Survey and Contact Department sent an agent to Lyff, a physician. All we can gather from his reports is that the Lyffans are human, which we already knew."

Master Control had plans for Lyff. "It is anticipated, as I said before, that the enemy's first major attack will be launched in about ten years against Lyff. The Federation will not have sufficient naval power to defend Lyff, however, so your job will be to prepare Lyff to defend herself. Is that clear?"

"I have a few questions, sir."

"Go ahead, John."

"First, how many men are you assigning to this project?"

"You three, plus the doctor who is already there."

"Four men? Then, how nearly ready is Lyff now, sir?

I mean, how large a space fleet does Lyff have? How about weapons? Are there—"

"Stop. I see that I haven't made the assignment clear yet. The Lyffan culture is what you might call pre-technical. Unaided, Lyff might manage to produce an internal combustion motor some time in the next hundred years."

"I see. And what are we supposed to do?"

"From internal combustion to space flight is usually a matter of from eighty to a hundred and twenty-five years. Your job is to reduce the total period of development to less than a decade. If possible, you are to do this without unduly disrupting the Lyffan economy. Master Control says you have a fifty-fifty chance of success. Personally, I believe—" He was interrupted by a high-pitched bell. "Ah, your ship is ready. We're sending you out on the old *Andrew Blake*. The trip will take twenty-four days, gentlemen, which should give you time enough to plan your campaign. I wish you luck and Godspeed, gentlemen." Bellman was an old-line Navy man.

4

"As far as I'm concerned," Harlen said, "Hurd's one of the crew. After all, he knows the city intimately, he knows his way around both the Court and the underworld, even though he's well-educated he knows how to deal with the commoners, he's fought beside me, and he knows enough about us to give us a hard time if we turn him out." It was the morning after Harlen's adventure, and Special Detail L-2 was meeting in Doctor Jellfte's office to decide the fate of Hurd Gar-Olnyn Saarlip.

Hurd was waiting in the kitchen, wholly unaware that the conversation in the office concerned him. He had given up trying to understand what these strange people were up to. They were crazy, obviously. All of them. Even his good but oddly-named friend John, with whom he had killed, Mother protect us, two whole noblemen—even John was crazy. Even John. "Federation," indeed. "Terra!" "Educational tapes!" Bah! Half of what these people said was meaningless noise, baby talk. Crazy, all of them.

"But look, John," Pindar Smith was being annoyingly rational, "how do you know we can trust this man? You must admit that he's nothing but a criminal, for all of his rhyme and rhythm. What's to keep him from turning us in the minute we upset some nobleman enough to get a price put on our heads?"

Ansgar, the journalist, answered that one. "Good Lord, Pin," he said. "I don't think you studied this culture at all. What were you doing on the trip out while the rest of us were in the hypno tanks?" Smith didn't answer. "Look,"

Sorenstein went on, "this native friend of John's killed two noblemen and let a third one get away alive."

He let a small silence form, and then continued. "According to Lyffan theology, all nobles are delegated by Mother to serve as Fathers in one degree or another. For anyone but a higher noble to injure one of them is blasphemy, and the penalty is death—something they call Mother's Wrath. To kill a nobleman is sacrilege, and they have a special punishment for it. They call it The Long Death, because it takes a whole month. And this fellow Hurd killed two, count them, two highly placed nobles with beards down to their sacred belly buttons. And John is the other witness."

"That's right," Jellfte added. "Killing a noble is a sacrilege." He sounded as though he half believed it. "Saarlip'd rather kill himself quickly and be done with it than lose Lieutenant Harlen's friendship."

Apropos of which, a full Embrace of Mother's Guards, two hundred heavily armed Lyffans, was marching through Lyffdarg. Tchornyo Gar-Spolnyen Hiirlte, First Son and Heritor of Spoln Gar-Tchornyen Hiirlte, Grand Duke of Lyff and Heriditary Sponsor of the Guild of Fabric Makers, not to mention several other equally imposing titles, strode at the head of the Embrace. Behind him walked an acolyte of the Guild of Proclaimers. A long, narrow oval of silence moved with the Embrace, and into this oval at every street corner the acolyte proclaimed:

All Lyffans must pay heed to this! All Lyffans must pay heed to this! In Mother's Hidden Name, so be it spoken. Mother's hatred is proclaimed against two unknown men of common birth who last night basely wounded and most treacherously slew by cowardly devices the noble sons of two most noble families.

A penance of six days is now proclaimed.

Let there be sold neither meat nor wine nor beer within the Darg of Lyff. Let no music sound, and let

26

there be no laughter. This upon pain of Mother's Gentle Discipline.

Let every man of Lyffdarg offer prayers at the Temple daily with the rising and the falling of Mother's Eye. This upon pain of Mother's Gentle Discipline.

For six days shall the city gates be closed. Let no man leave or enter Lyffdarg until the penance is accomplished. This upon pain of Mother's Gentle Discipline.

All Lyffans must pay heed to this! In Mother's Hidden Name, so be it spoken. Mother's Wrath is heavy on the sacrilegious murderers, and they shall endure The Long Death, and for them there shall be no place of comfort.

Pay heed to this! In Mother's Name. Whosoever shall deliver these men, one or both, to Mother's Embrace shall be enobled and made wealthy, and whosoever shall shield them from Mother's Embrace shall partake in equal measure of their dying. It has been proclaimed. In Mother's Hidden Name, so be it spoken.

Then the Embrace and its oval of silence moved on. And all the while Tchornyo, who was already being called "The Survivor" in noble circles, eyed the Lyffan crowds suspiciously, ready to cry out the moment he saw either of his last night's enemies.

"All right then," Smith conceded, "this pickpocket is our first recruit. But do we have to tell him *everything*?"

Over Smith's vigorous protest, it was agreed that Hurd had to be told everything indeed, and as often as might prove necessary to make him understand. "He's not just a native guide," Harlen insisted. "We're going to have to enlist him in the Navy, put him in the chain of command, and make him a full partner in the project. Otherwise we won't be able to make efficient use of his knowledge and experience. He'll always to be telling us what he thinks we'd like to hear unless he knows exactly what we're up to—My God, I just thought of something!"

Sorenstein smiled knowingly, and the others asked in ragged unision, "What?"

The journalist answered instead of John. "Hurd," he said, "is about to become the only enlisted man on Lyff."

Lyff's only enlisted-man-to-be was at that moment enjoying a gastronomic orgy in the doctor's kitchen. Hurd hadn't seen such food since his patron baron's death, and since he fully expected to join his patron soon, he was not content merely to look at the shelves upon crowded shelves of luxury foods. By the time John Harlen came to get him, Hurd had eaten enough food to keep a peasant family well-fed for a week. The Lyffan poet was bloated, sluggish, deliriously happy and willing to accept whatever fate Mother might decide to send him.

"Hurd, old son," said John, "we'd like to talk to you."

Hurd burped joyfully, dragged himself to his feet and waddled down the hall behind his Terran friend.

The madmen, as Hurd thought of them, occupied armchairs drawn around in a semicircle focused on a high, wooden stool. The armchairs were in darkness but the stool was brightly lighted. Hurd was uncomfortably reminded of a confessional chamber at the Temple. He'd been questioned once, back when he was still a law-abiding and respectable poet, and he'd never been able to forget the experience, even though the priests were careful not to leave any marks and apologized afterward. It had been worse than Mother's Gentle Discipline, which was a relatively simple matter of flogging.

"Please sit on the stool, Hurd," said a voice—not John's, and Mother alone knew whose—from the darkness. Struggling awkwardly with his unaccustomed weight, Hurd sat.

"Hurd Gar-Olnyn Saarlip," said another voice, "it is true, is it not, that you killed two noblemen of Lyff last night? Answer yes or no."

"Well," Hurd said nervously, "last night's affair might

be construed in such a manner, I suppose. Yes." He was not enjoying this any more than he was understanding it. He wished he were in any one of several other places.

"Hurd Gar-Olnyn Saarlip, murderer of noblemen," came a bass voice deeper than doom, the doctor's, obviously, "have you perhaps forgotten that I, Tarn Gar-Terrayen Jellfte, am an ordained Duke of Lyff?"

Everything that Hurd had eaten turned to stone within him. "Your Worship," he whined, "I swear it was really an error, mistaken identity caused by the darkness, which led me to think they were common-born robbers attacking Lord John under cover of night, Oh Most Reverend Duke, Sire, wherefore I defended . . ." Hurd's anapestic groveling ran down into silence. He sat motionless on the cruelly lighted stool, too hot and too cold and sweating in terror, and waited for Mother's Guards to seize him.

The stillness stretched, and stretched, and stretched, and finally, just before Hurd was going to break, the silence broke. Insofar as he could be, Hurd was glad for this. With so little left him anyhow, he'd have hated falling apart in front of these strange people. He couldn't imagine himself doing it in a dignified manner.

It was John's voice that broke the silence. "Relax, old son," he said kindly, "we're not going to turn you in."

Hurd wept and blubbered in shameful gratitude. John politely ignored him and went on talking. "We just wanted to be sure you knew what you were up against. Don't worry about it. Now we want to explain a few things so that you'll understand what's happening. Do you think you're ready to follow some simple explanations?"

Hurd wiped away his tears, or most of them, firmed his jaw, and nodded.

"Great," John said heartily. "You're first, Ansgar."

Ansgar Sorenstein spoke slowly and clearly. His voice was almost hypnotic in quality, and Hurd was certain he could fall asleep listening if he were given only the very slightest additional encouragement. "Lyff," Ansgar said, "is the fourth of eleven planets that move around Mother's

Eye in roughly egg-shaped paths. Mother's Eye is a star, pretty much like most of the stars you see in the sky at night. Mother's Eye seems to be brighter than the other stars only because it is so close to Lyff. Many of the other stars are really much brighter than Mother's Eye, but they are very far away from Lyff, so far away that we measure their distance by the number of years it takes for their light to reach Lyff, and even so the numbers are uncomfortably large. There are millions of millions of such stars, and around thousands of thousands of them planets very much like Lyff move in roughly egg-shaped paths." He gave Hurd a twenty-minute lesson in astronomy that stretched the poet's mind as nothing ever had before, stretched it until it encompassed a galaxy. Hurd forgot his personal fears in an almost religious perception of the physical universe.

"And there," Sorenstein concluded, "so far away that its light cannot be seen from Lyff, is the sun that we have called Sol. It is more like Mother's Eye than most stars are. Planets move around Sol exactly as Lyff moves around Mother's Eye. Of these planets, we have named the third Terra. It is a planet almost exactly like Lyff, and it is our home. We are called Terrans, just as you are called Lyffans, and we have traveled from our home to yours."

There was a pause while Hurd assimilated all he had been told. Everyone could see how his face gleamed with the wonder and beauty of it. Then John asked quietly, "Do you understand what Ansgar said?"

After another pause, Hurd answered. "Yes, I understand," he said, "and it is wonderful. In *The Book of Garth Gar-Muyen Garth*, which is Mother's Law, are written many strange things, hard to understand, that now have been made clear to me. The Holy Garth, whom Mother loves, described the place of comfort Mother has created for her children, calling it The Third World, Beautiful, Our Promised Home."

"Great," said John. "I don't think we need theology right now, though. Your turn, Pin."

Pindar Smith cleared his throat self-consciously and began. "Twenty-five hundred Terran years ago, or almost thirty Lyffan lifetimes ago, if you prefer, life on Terra was very much like life is today on Lyff. Transportation was very poor, and a journey of more than a few miles was a hazardous undertaking. There were few machines, and most of them were musical instruments. Communication between distant places could only be carried on in writing, and depended, of course, upon the uncertain transportation facilities then available.

"Diseases swept unchecked across the planet in vast epidemic waves, killing or crippling millions of people. The land was divided into many little nations, most of which were at war most of the time. A few people were very wealthy and almost everybody else was very poor, and hunger killed nearly as many people as disease did.

"This time was called, much later, the Baroque Period, and there were many men then and during the centuries following who thought it was the golden age of Terra, not because it was comfortable or enlightened or any of the things we'd expect a golden age to be, but partially because for any age in history there are always men then and afterward who think of it as an ideal time, and partially because the forces that brought Terra to its present position were, for the most part, first set in motion during the Baroque Period. Ideas had been gathering on Terra for many centuries, and in that time, at last, men began to translate their hoard of ideas into deeds. The spirits of invention and synthesis reached their first full vigor during that time."

Smith talked on in his dry voice, halting now and then to clear his throat again. He described the history of Terra from the days of Frederick the Great and the legendary J. S. Bach to the present in terms of invention (the translation of ideas into objects and deeds) and synthesis (the combination of apparently unrelated ideas to produce new

31

ideas and inventions). Hurd listened intently, but he was frequently confused.

Finally Pindar Smith said, "And that is part of the reason we Terrans are on Lyff. Your world is still baroque, and we have been ordered to lead you through the progress we took twenty-five hundred years to make, and to do it in no more than ten years."

After a shorter pause than before, John asked dubiously, "Is that all clear, old son?"

"Alas," Hurd replied, "I'm afraid it is not. The history of Terra is much more confusing than the workings of the galaxy."

The Terrans laughed loudly, confusing Hurd still more. Then John said, "That's all right, Hurd. I'm not too sure Pindar really understands it either. As soon as you learn to read Terran, I'll lend you some books that might help. Now it's Doctor Jellfte's turn. Are you ready, sir?"

The doctor's voice was very deep and strong. He described the development of transportation from the coach and four of baroque days to the faster-than-light spacecraft of the present. In the course of this, he also described the evolution of the Terran Federation. Jellfte wasn't quite as confusing as Smith had been, but Hurd hoped his good friend John would also lend him some books about the history of transportation.

During the transportation lecture, the Embrace, having made the rounds of all but the noble sections of Lyffdarg, returned to the Guard Barracks at the Temple. The acolyte of the Guild of Proclaimers had made his last six announcements in a hoarse, dry whisper, much to the dismay of the Lyffdargers, who were required by Mother's Law to know and obey the contents of every proclamation, whether they'd heard it or not.

Tchornyo Gar-Spolnyen Hiirlte, First Son *et cetera,* was tired and irritable. He'd wasted the whole Mother-lorn day staring at commoners, and, of course, being stared back at by the same commoners. Not that he much minded being stared at. Even for a Lyffan noble he was unusually handsome, as he well knew, and it was not unpleasant to see others taking note of that fact. He was almost two and a half arm lengths tall and imperially slim. Like most Lyffans, his hair was so blond it was nearly white, but it was longer, straighter, cleaner, and more light-textured than most, for he spent more time caring for it than most Lyffans could afford. And his beard, which was his own and not a fake, as poor, dead, stupid Garlyn's had been, that affected son of a Dalber!—Anyway, his beard matched his hair in all respects, and majestically fell to his waist, a full half-finger longer than the next longest beard among his friends. Tchornyo hoped that beards would remain in style a good long time. He was justly proud of his, and he'd hate to have to shave it off.

Only, his beard and hair were dusty now, coated with dust from his futile all-day peasant-staring expedition. Dusty! Sweet Mother, they were actually dirty! And dull and heavy from the dirt. Tchornyo suspected it would take a fairly strong wind to make his hair stir gently now. Mother forsake those filthy assassins! And the filthy commoners, as well, and all their filthy dirt.

With his blue eyes flashing frozen fire, Tchornyo Gar-Spolnyen Hiirlte mounted his blooded dalbler and rode toward home at a speed that endangered every pedestrian en route. He'd have to attend the prayer meeting at dusk, and before then he'd Mother-well have to wash his Mother-lorn hair. Forsake and crush those Mother-hating murderers anyhow!

Doctor Jellfte's history of transportation was followed by a discussion by Pindar Smith of what machines Lyff's culture could be considered ready to produce. "Most important," he said, "are farming implements. Improved plows, hoes, rakes, spades, and scythes can easily be introduced before the next sowing season without noticeable cultural upheaval. Agriculture must be raised as far above the mere subsistence level as possible before any really major innovations are introduced. You can't establish industries until you have an agricultural surplus to support them. After all," he chuckled, "you can't expect your iron workers to eat iron." Smith was affecting an accent none of his friends could identify, which he fondly imagined to be twentieth-century American Southern. It was quaint, but not at all convincing.

"Thank you, Pin," John Harlen interrupted when he noticed that Smith was about to launch into an involved comparative analysis of metal-tempering techniques. "How much of that did you understand, Hurd?"

"Almost all, I think, friend John. The machines are unfamiliar, but the principles are clear enough."

John was struck with admiration. "You amaze me, Hurd," he said warmly. "You've sat on that stool for two and a half hours now, while we've been throwing enormous doses of information at you as foreign to your own experience as anything *could* be, completely alien data, and yet you've managed to understand just about everything we've said. You know, most Terrans, myself included, would have overloaded their circuits and blown their fuses long ago under such treatment. I don't think any of us here could absorb more than an hour's worth of such totally alien information, and there you sit, unfazed and eager for more."

"But I'm not completely unprepared. *The Book of Garth—*"

"That's all right, old son. It won't take us long to finish this. Only two more lectures, and then we can all go and eat. Now it's Doc Jellfte's turn again."

"Thank you," the doctor said. Hurd was beginning to think of the nobleman's rumbling voice as friendly rather than ominous. He hadn't thought of a nobleman as being friendly since his patron baron died.

"Twelve years ago, the Survey and Contact Department of the Terran Federation stationed me on Lyff. My job was to carry out a survey of Lyffan culture and to influence its development in such a way that the planet could eventually be incorporated into the Federation with as little inconvenience to the Lyffan people as possible. At that time this was considered a long-range project, and I didn't expect to live to witness its completion.

"The Federation's policy has always been to avoid overt contact with undeveloped cultures, for experience has shown that such contact invariably destroys the lower culture, leaving the Federation with the messy and often bloody job of rehabilitating an entire planetary population. Thus the Federation only makes overt contact with cultures that have developed space travel, because a civilization that can build its own spaceships isn't likely to fall apart when it learns of the higher civilization of the Terran Federation. Indeed, there seems to be an equation of some sort between space flight and cultural maturity. This equation doesn't hold up under logical analysis, but until recently it has worked out quite nicely in practice.

"Anyhow, when an inhabited planet is discovered, the Federation sends secret agents, such as myself, to it, and these agents work to accelerate the natural maturation rate of the indigenous culture. If this confuses you, Hurd, don't worry about it. Lieutenant Harlen will explain it better later.

"I have been endeavoring to accelerate the Lyffan maturation by introducing, very gradually, advanced medical concepts. The formula involved is quite simple. Improved medicine results in lower death rates, higher birth rates, longer lives and, eventually, population pressure. These things, especially population pressure, combine to force increasingly rapid progress on a culture—either that, or wars and cultural suicide, which are rare and can be dealt with by other agencies of the Federation. My pet project was to have a medical school that would eventually develop into an academy of science, but the Special Detail has made that project obsolete.

"According to the plan I was working from, Lyff would have developed space flight in about two hundred years, an incredibly short time, as such things go. But now Lieutenant Harlen and his group are here to push your people into space within a decade, and I'll let him explain how and why."

John Harlen stood up, the only speaker to have done so, and moved into the circle of light Hurd had been occupying alone. "It seems," he said grimly, "that the Federation is no longer alone in the galaxy.

"The Federation is a free and peaceful association of sentient beings. It's called the Terran Federation only because we Terrans started it. Most of the member races aren't even vaguely humanoid, which is to say, Hurd, that they don't look anything like you and me. I won't try to describe any of them, but someday you'll meet some. There are a very few humanoid races that look more like you and me than they look like anything else, but they're pretty obviously not humans.

"Now this business of human or nonhuman doesn't really matter. The important thing is that all these wildly various races have been able to communicate with each other, to work and live in harmony with each other. Contact with a new intelligent race has always lead to communication. There have been problems, sure, but none of them impossible to solve.

"But now there's a new race moving into the galaxy from Mother knows where. We know they're intelligent and have space flight, because we've only encountered them in spaceships, but that's just about all we know about them. They don't communicate, they don't allow contact. They shoot on sight and either kill or get killed. We've never run across a race like this before, so we have to play pretty much by ear, which is not really the best way to do this sort of thing.

"Anyhow, the only other thing we know about these strangers is that they're moving into this galaxy, and they're due to reach Lyff in about ten years, more or less. Preferably more. We don't know for sure what they'll do when they get here, but they seem to like to kill things."

There was a long pause while Hurd assimilated this new data. John paced back and forth within the circle of light. Finally Hurd sighed heavily and said, "These strangers don't seem to be very good people."

John hurried on. "Right. That's why we're here with our ten-year crash program. We must have a fighting force on hand when the strangers arrive, and the best way to get the force we need is to build it from scratch right here on Lyff. Of course, we'll have to make a lot of changes in the, ah, Lyffan Way of Life, but the computers back home say our program will work, and if it does, you Lyffans will have a chance to defend yourselves and to join the Federation."

"That sounds like a sales talk, friend John. I've heard the same thing on the Street of Merchants hundreds of times. But what happens if your program doesn't work?"

"Well . . ." John hesitated. He hadn't expected Hurd to be so acute. "Yes," he went on bravely, "if the program doesn't work . . ." This time he paused for emphasis. "Lyff will be destroyed, either by the Lyffans or by the strangers, but most likely by both."

Another silence. Mother's Eye was falling, and from all over Lyffdarg men were shuffling toward the Temple to do penance. Prayers had to be offered in the vast amphitheater, usually reserved for the spring and autumn Great Festivals, in order to accommodate all of Lyffdarg's men. Only one gate was open, and the Lyffans pushed through it six abreast, scattering when they were inside to reach the seats assigned to their neighborhoods and to register with their neighborhood priests.

Tchornyo Gar-Spolnyen Hiirlte, his hair still damp and his temper still frayed, was watching the arriving worshipers from a cramped balcony over the open gate. He was becoming thoroughly sick and weary of staring at unwashed commoners. His honorable father, Spoln Gar-

Tchornyen Hiirlte, was with him to provide moral support, and the fresh Embrace of Mother's Guards herding the worshipers through the gate supplied an even greater welcome and a more practical kind of support.

"Are you *sure* you can identify them, boy?" the elder Hiirlte queried anxiously.

"Oh Mother's nose, Daddy! Of *course* I can identify them. I'll *never* forget those evil, common faces."

Hiirlte Senior knew better than to continue the discussion while his son was being petulant.

"Now, old son," John said cheerfully, "we have arrived at the crux of the matter, which is this: Will you join us?"

"Join you?"

"Yes."

"How do you mean 'join'?"

"All the way. Join Special Detail L-2, join the Federation Navy, which will automatically make you the first Lyffan to join the Federation. Be a full partner in the project and help us usher Lyff into the Space Age, or else die with us if we fail."

Hurd stood up for the first time in more than three hours. He looked slowly around the darkened semicircle, imagining the faces he couldn't quite see. Then he spoke. "In common words, you're asking me to help you tear my world apart, to bring to ruin all the things that I have known throughout my life. You're asking me to help destroy the culture that created me. You want me to betray my race, my nation and my planet. I have lived in what you want me to destroy for twenty-five years, and love my world above my own dear life—Of course I'll join you. Why did you wait so long to ask me?"

The induction ceremony was simple but impressive, and Hurd was promised that as soon as he could read it, he'd be given a copy of the Constitution he'd just sworn to uphold. Then Special Detail L-2 and the only enlisted man on Lyff went to supper. It had been a good day.

5

"The first thing we need is a shop," Ansgar said.

"A shop? What for? We don't have anything to sell yet. Why do we need a shop?" Pindar Smith was busily being a businessman.

"I think that Ansgar means a workshop," John said quietly. He was used to these three-way conversations, and resigned to playing the role of clarifier whenever they took place.

"That's right," Ansgar said excitedly, "a workshop. We've been on this God-forsaken planet—"

"Mother-lorn," John corrected. That was another of his roles.

"Sorry. We've been on this Mother-lorn planet now for three weeks and we haven't accomplished a thing. We've got to start inventing stuff, and we need a shop to invent in. That's all there is to it."

"Okay, okay. I'll go along with you," Smith said, "but what the hell are we going to invent?"

"Mother's nose, Pin," John interjected. "Where have you been? I thought you were with us when we decided on the telegraph."

"Why in Mother's Hidden Name are we going to invent the telegraph? Sometimes—"

John stood up wearily and checked the reasons off on his fingers. "One: telegraph involves electricity; two: electricity leads to electronics; three: telegraph involves wires; four: wires lead to advanced metallurgy; five: telegraph requires a school for training telegraphers; six: school leads to universal literacy; seven: telegraph means rapid communication; eight: rapid communication leads to newspapers; nine: newspapers give us a chance to play propaganda; ten: telegraph company requires guards; I've run out of fingers, but eleven: guards can very quickly become the core of a standing army." He sat down again. "Oh yes," he added, "I forgot one. Twelve: Lyffan technology is just barely advanced enough so that we can invent the telegraph without disrupting the whole Motherlorn culture. Any more questions?"

"Okay," Smith conceded, "so we rent a shop. How?"

Renting a shop on Lyff was much like renting a shop on Terra. Hurd and John made a long, hot, haggling tour of the business district of Lyffdarg, searching for vacancies.

"The important thing to remember, old son, is that we want the lowest rent possible. If people get the idea that we're big spenders, we'll have every eye in the city on us and we won't be able to get anything done. We've got to be inconspicuous."

They finally found a place that would suit them on Lame Dalber Street, right next door to a tavern. Even John, who was used to Terran architecture, had to admit that the building was impressive. Most of the buildings in Lyffdarg were squat things made of plaster, lathes, and heavy, hand-hewn timbers and roofed over with something he thought was called wattle, unless wattles were those funny red things extinct Terran birds were supposed to have had. He'd have to ask Ansgar about wattles.

But the Lame Dalber Street building was impressive, and there wasn't a wattle in sight, no matter what wattles were. It was built entirely of a gleaming white stone to be found nowhere else in the city, and it was four stories high, a veritable skyscraper.

"It used to belong to the Temple," the landlord said in a confidential tone. "The Little Sisters lived here." He sniggered. "That is how it is that I can rent so sound a building at so ridiculous a low rate."

40

"But we only want the ground floor," John said.

"What do you call a ridiculous low rate?" asked Hurd.

Since Hurd was, logically enough, handling the negotiations, it was him the landlord answered. "A trivial nothing," he burbled. "Only ninety-seven dalbers a month."

"I thought so," Hurd said. "Come along, friend John, let's go someplace where no one will try to rob us."

"But that's not much," John said. Then he caught on. "Of course," he continued, "it's a good deal more than we can afford, but for a building like this it's not much. I hope you can rent it someday, landlord. Goodbye."

They stood up and started to leave. "Wait, wait," the landlord said. "Because you are new to our city, for no other reason, and because Mother loves a bargain, just for you I charge only ninety dalbers. How is that?"

"Umm," Hurd said. "That's very kind of you, sir, but we must be going now." Whereupon Hurd and John sat down again and started to haggle.

Next door, in the Lame Dalber Tavern, Tchornyo GarSpolnyen Hiirlte was becoming maudlin drunk. In the past three weeks he'd developed a case of chronic insomnia even the King's Own Physician was powerless to cure. He couldn't forget the way the killer had laughed at poor old Garlyn's false beard.

"It's a plot," he insisted between sips of wine. "The commoners are rising against us. They want to overthrow the government! *They don't love Mother!*"

He was drinking alone. Two weeks ago his friends had stopped calling him "The Survivor" and started calling him "The Drigol," a name that could mean "wet blanket," "party pooper," or "old maid," as the context demanded. At any rate, he was drinking alone, with no one to listen to his warnings but the tavernkeeper, who was growing annoyed.

"One more glass wine," he whispered to his wife. "Just one more glass wine I sell that Mother-lorn drunk, then nobleman or no nobleman, I throw the son of a dalber out my bar!"

"Fifty-one dalbers, gentlemen. I can go no lower." The landlord was sweating profusely. "Already you are taking the food out of my family's mouths."

"Tavernkeeper, more wine," Tchornyo shouted next door.

"I don't know," John said dubiously. "How does that strike you, Hurd?"

"It seems reasonable, I suppose."

"Look, buddy," said the tavernkeeper, "I think maybe you had too much already, so how about I give you this glass wine on the house, eh? And you drink it up and go home, hah?"

"Now, gentlemen, if you'll just sign here—You do know how to write, don't you?" The landlord was eager to close the deal before John and Hurd could start haggling again.

"Mother's nose!" John exclaimed. "Look, Hurd, he had the lease made out before we even got here."

"This happens," Hurd said. "Let's sign the Mother-lorn thing and go home. I'm weary to the middle of my bones."

They signed the lease, traded expressions of good will and friendship with the landlord, and returned to the hot and brightly lighted street. While they were standing outside their new building, letting their eyes adjust to the sunlight, they heard a disturbance from the tavern next door.

"I don't care you are whose son, get out from my place you Mother-lorn drunk!" a deep voice shouted.

"You dalberson Mother-hater," a higher voice shouted. "I'm going to bring my friends here tonight, yes I am. You'll be sorry. You're part of the plot, that's what you are."

There was a struggle at the tavern door, and then a colorfully dressed young man was picking himself up from the pavement while a more drably dressed tavern-keeper stalked back into his establishment.

"That fellow looks familiar," John whispered.

"Yes. Where have we— Oh yes, I remember now."

Tchornyo, having regained his feet, was brushing the dust off his clothes with ineffectual gestures and staring angrily around the street to see who had witnessed his humiliation. John and Hurd were trying to tiptoe away. It took Tchornyo's wine-soaked memory a few seconds to recognize the two tiptoers, whom he'd seen last in near darkness, but once recognition was sure, action followed promptly.

"You!" Tchornyo shouted.

"Oh Mother," Hurd muttered. "We've had it." They broke into a run.

"Murderers," Tchornyo yelled. He started unsteadily down the street after them.

"Faster, friend John, faster."

"What's happening out here?" yelled the tavernkeeper from his door.

"Those are the men," Tchornyo answered. He pointed forward at John and Hurd, who were rapidly approaching a corner, and looked back at the tavernkeeper. At once he stumbled on an ill-laid cobblestone and fell roughly on his stomach.

"Mother-lorn drunks," the tavernkeeper said, retreating to the comfortable darkness of his inn.

"Stop those men," Tchornyo yelled as he got to his feet again. "A reward to whoever stops those men." He ran down the street, staggering the width of it as he ran.

John and Hurd turned the corner. "For a drunk," John panted, "that boy sure can run."

"This is," Hurd gasped, "no time for," panting, "conversation."

Tchornyo rounded the corner and charged down on them like an irregular act of nature. The stagger he had established on Lame Dalber Street was too wide for the narrow side street, and the first thing of any significance Tchornyo managed to do was knock over a merchant's display of earthenware cooking utensils.

"Ai!" the merchant shouted as the earthenware goods shattered on the cobbles. "Ai!" echoed the merchant's wife as her husband ran, slipping and sliding through the shards, after Tchornyo.

Now, to the young nobleman, the sound of smashing crockery meant nothing. The clatter of the merchant's stock fragmenting on the cobblestones was just a common noise to Tchornyo, nothing more. And the merchant himself, weaving back and forth down the street behind Tchornyo and yelling incoherently, was not an angry pursuer, he was an ally. Tchornyo drew his sword and waved it in the air to encourage the merchant.

"Mother protect us," the merchant shouted to his neighbors, "the madman has a sword! We'll all be killed!"

And his wife yelled, from the safety of the shop, "Stop him! Thief! Stop him!"

Tchornyo risked another backward glance. Good. There were lots of people helping him now. The killers were as good as caught. With this thought, he lurched into a carefully heaped pyramid of field melons and sent the hard-shelled, globular fruit rolling every which way across the street.

"Our friend," John said, "is having a little," in short gasps, "trouble."

"Mother loves us," was all Hurd had breath to respond.

They turned another corner and entered the dalber market. The dalber is a most unsteady beast. Sometime during the course of Lyffan evolution, a medium-sized lizard could not make up its mind whether it wanted to be a pterodactyl or a dinosaur. The result was a dalber, the most skittish beast of burden in the galaxy.

There was a herd of more than three hundred dalbers for sale in the market that day. As John and Hurd dashed by, the beasts became nervous, and their usual bright green color faded at once to a skittery chartreuse. Something, the dalbers thought, was definitely amiss. The situation, they were convinced, was getting out of claw and required close scrutiny, instant action, and as little cogitation as possible. The dalbers bunched together for protection, causing their drover, who knew more about dalbers than he liked, to swear flamboyantly.

When John and Hurd were halfway up the block, Tchornyo Gar-Spolnyen Hiirlte turned the corner, shrilling loudly, waving his sword dangerously, and in every way possible confirming the dalbers' assessment of the situation. And behind him, weaving from side to side as he wove, shouting as he shouted and running like overwrought madmen, came a horde of angry merchants.

The drover's swearing faded imperceptibly into devout prayers. He knew dalbers. The beasts, on the other hand, said Gronch! like a herd of amplified geese. Their color changed from skittery chartreuse to horrified yellow, and they were instantly smitten with a desperate urge to get away from this nameless peril.

As if on a signal, three hundred gronching dalbers stampeded. The drover prayed in vain while chasing them.

"Murderers!" Tchornyo bellowed.

"Gronch! Gronch!" shrieked three hundred hysterical dalbers behind him.

Behind the dalbers ran the drover, screaming about unprintable parts of Mother's holy anatomy.

Behind the drover a streetful of merchants shouted, "Stop him! Stop that man!"

An off-duty Guardsman, loitering in a doorway, watched with amazement as the procession flew past him. As the drover passed, the Guardsman heard the merchants' shouting. His reflexes were lightning fast. He leaped out of the doorway and tackled the drover. The Guardsman and the drover fell to the ground, and the merchants ran heavily across the bodies without even noticing they were there.

Tchornyo risked another backward glance. Mother's nose! What were all those Mother-lorn dalbers—Umpfh!

Lyffdarg cobblestones tend to be uneven.

John and Hurd made a quick right turn. The dalbers, ignoring Tchornyo completely except to tred on him in passing, ran straight ahead, down the street and toward the Temple. Before Tchornyo could pick his dalber-buffetted body off the ground, the dealer in earthenware cooking utensils caught up with him and saved him the trouble.

"Two hundred earthenware frying pans," the merchant snarled, shaking Tchornyo like a polishing cloth. "Forty-nine large earthenware pots for making stew." He was slapping Tchornyo's face. Tchornyo, alas, was crying.

"Four hundred field melons," another merchant insisted, kicking Tchornyo's shins as he spoke.

"Three hundred Mother-lorn dalbers," proclaimed the bruised and bleeding drover. In one hand he held his dalber whip, and in the other he held a small cobblestone.

"Here, here," said the Guard roughly. "I'll take care of this. Come along, you." He grabbed Tchornyo's collar and dragged him off toward the Temple.

"But I'm a nobleman," Tchornyo wept. "You let the killers get away."

"Mother-lorn drunk," muttered the tavernkeeper, who had been attracted by the noise.

"By the way, friend John," Hurd said as they walked tiredly home, "have I ever told you the joke about the dalber who wanted to sing?"

"No, friend Hurd, I don't believe you have."

"Well, once upon a time there was this dalber . . ."

"All right, bring him in," rumbled Spoln Gar-Tchornyen Hiirlte. The old man was most angry.

"Daddy," Tchornyo whined as he entered his father's study, "you don't understand. I was—"

"You are absolutely correct. I do *not* understand. Furthermore, I *will* not understand. So far today I have had to pay for some two hundred and seventy-five earthenware utensils of dubious value and enormous price, some five hundred field melons I had no opportunity to eat, and some four hundred dalbers of no doubt worthless breeds, though I paid thoroughbred money for them. The damage the dalbers caused has not been estimated yet, but I will doubtless have to pay for that as well."

"But Daddy—"

"Quiet. That is not why I am angry. I will merely subtract today's expenses from your allowance. I am angry because I, a Grand Duke of Lyff, had to walk to the Temple this afternoon—walk, mind you—and humble myself before some common clod of a Guard Captain in order to secure the release of my son, my only son, from a common felons' cell."

"But Daddy—"

"Will you be quiet! You are a disgrace. You have disgraced your family names, all three of them. You have furthermore disgraced yourself, an accomplishment that borders on impossibility. Worst of all, you have disgraced me. I am ashamed to go to the palace. I am ashamed even to receive delegations from the Guild of Fabric Makers. Do you understand that? I am now ashamed to face mere commoners. Oh . . . Tchornyo, if I had another son I'd disown you right now. Go away from me, you drunken fool. Go to your room and pray for forgiveness, or common sense: whatever it is that you lack. I don't want to have to look at you for a while."

Dirty, ragged, bleeding, and thoroughly humiliated, Tchornyo backed fearfully away from his father's desk, bowing at every third step. With his third bow, he knocked over a large, decorative vase.

"Idiot!"

Tchornyo turned and ran, weeping, down the long hall to his own room. There he sat for seven Mother-lorn hours swearing vengeance, vengeance, vengeance.

6

"Walsh?" Admiral Bellman was indignant. "What the devil does that old fogey want?"

"Shh," the Admiral's yeoman cautioned. "He's right outside, sir."

"You're wrong, young man. I'm right in here," said the high-pitched nasal voice that had bored three generations of newstape men to near catatonia while terrifying three generations of civil servants.

"Why, Emsley Walsh," the Admiral burbled with instant enthusiasm. "It's good to see you."

"Don't give me that line, Edvalt. If it was good to see me I wouldn't be here." After fifty years in Parliament, Senator Walsh simply refused to be unnecessarily polite. "You'd better clear out, sonny," he told the nervous yeoman. "Your boss and I have things to talk about."

As Walsh sat down and prepared to make himself comfortable and Bellman miserable with an evil-smelling ten credit cigar, the yeoman skittered gratefully back to his desk in the outer office. "All right, Bellman," the senator said as soon as the office door was closed, "what's all this noise I've been hearing about you people and a contact violation?"

Emsley Walsh, Senior Senator from Australia and long-time Senate Majority Leader, was a desiccated, pencil-thin, eighty-five-year-old relic of a man. He would have looked like everybody's great-grandfather, were it not for his burning eyes and the dedicated way his skin was stretched drum-tight across his skull. As founder and leader of the popular Conservationist Party, he held nearly absolute power over everyone on the government's pay-roll, and he knew it.

"What do you mean, contact violation?" Bellman stalled.

"You know exactly what I mean," Walsh snapped. He then proceeded to describe in awesome detail Special Detail L-2, which was supposed to have been kept secret. "You know where we Consies stand," he continued. "This meddling in the affairs of an underprivileged culture is nothing more or less than exploitation. You're using those innocent people for your own purposes, Bellman, and that amounts to sheer slavery. I tell you, the Party won't put up with it."

The trouble with the Conservationist Party was its altruism. The Party was always acting for someone else's good, uninvited, and in the heat of its dedication to the underdog, the Party was always inventing underdogs that existed only in its own collective imagination. The Party's basic assumption, that whoever was in power was automatically in error, was completely unmodified by the fact that for the past thirty years the Party had controlled at least five-eighths of the vote in every Federation election. All power is evil but ours, they seemed to think.

Bellman was not completely unprepared for the Party's sudden interest in Special Detail L-2. He'd hoped that standard security measures would serve to keep the project secret, but he'd also developed a prudent armory of evasive measures to fall back on in case security broke down. He used one of these emergency measures now, a full set of neatly forged documents that proved beyond all possible argument that there was no such thing as Special Detail L-2.

"That's where it stands, Senator," he finished bravely. "All of the Navy's resources are committed to the re-armament program. We just don't have men or ships to spare for this so-called Special Detail. We have a battle fleet to build, Senator, and that job doesn't leave us any time or energy to spare. Right now we couldn't commit a contact violation if we wanted to. But don't take my word for it, Senator. Here are the figures, take them home and study them. Every man and every piece of equipment is accounted for, with none left over to carry out this Special Detail you've been told about. You've probably been misled by some unusually plausible crackpot, Senator. At any rate, there is no contact violation."

The senator examined Bellman's careful documents in silence. Bellman ventured a cautious smile. The old boy seemed to be convinced.

Finally Emsley Walsh looked up from the papers and smiled benignly. "Bull," he said gently. "This," rattling the papers, "is nothing but a pack of lies. I can't deny that it is a very clever pack of lies, but cleverness doesn't make it true."

Bellman tried to object. "But Senator—"

The senator raised his hand for silence and the Admiral's objections subsided. "The Conservationist Party has inarguable evidence that the Navy is tampering with an underprivileged and helpless culture. The source of our information has never been wrong before, and we have no reason to believe that he is wrong now. We know about your Special Detail, we know who is involved in it and what its purpose is supposed to be. The only thing we don't know is the name and location of the planet your Special Detail is planning to destroy so wantonly, but we can find that out easily enough. Someone is bound to volunteer the information, but if no one does volunteer, a parliamentary investigation can always force the information out of anyone who has it. In this case, that means you."

The senator rose and started to leave. "I don't think I need to list the various crimes you and your Special Detail are engaged in committing. They range all the way from falsifying official records—and I'm taking these papers with me for evidence—all the way from falsifying official records to premeditated xenocide. On your head be it, Bellman. Good day." And with that the surprisingly agile old man was gone.

Admiral Bellman, shocked, sat motionless for half an hour, suffering twinges from a previously unsuspected ulcer. For that half hour he allowed himself the luxury of being thoroughly sick of Special Detail L-2. Then he called in the officers in charge of naval intelligence and naval security and set to work combatting the Consie menace.

7

The task of inventing the telegraph fell, naturally, to Pindar Smith. It took him five weeks.

"If all I had to do was invent the Mother-lorn telegraph, there wouldn't be any problems worth mentioning," he said. "Any Terran schoolboy could do that. What bothered me was that I had to invent the *Lyffan* telegraph, the kind of telegraph a native Lyffan might be expected to produce. The Mother-lorn thing had to be a logical development from contemporary knowledge, and there *are* no logical developments possible from the Motherless contemporary knowledge."

Smith was exaggerating, of course. His problem was not that the prerequisite techniques did not exist, but that they existed in unexpected forms. For instance:

"I quit," he told John one day.

John was sympathetic. "What's your problem, old son?" he asked.

"Copper wire, that's what. No one in Lyffdarg knows how to make copper wire, and I don't know how to make a telegraph without it. Before I can invent the telegraph, I'm going to have to invent copper wire, and before I can invent that I'm going to have to invent some nonelectrical use for it, which may take years to do."

"We don't have years, Pin. Are you sure nobody knows how to make wire?"

"Positive. I've asked the Guild of Metal Workers, the Guild of Pipe Makers and even the Mother-lorn Guild of Jewelers. They all know what copper is, but none of them has ever heard of copper wire. I'm stumped."

"Pardon me," Hurd interrupted. "What is this copper wire you're hunting for?"

When John Harlen and Pindar Smith had managed, talking in tandem, to explain copper wire, Hurd said, "If what you want is metallic thread made out of copper, the Guild of Brocaders should be able to make it for you, and if they can't, they can tell you who can."

"Brocaders?" said Harlen and Smith in ragged unison.

"Of course. They use gold and silver thread for decorating garments, don't they? Whoever makes their silver thread should be able to make copper thread, too."

After that Smith's task became much simpler. He made a list of the things he needed and gave Hurd the job of finding them. This lead to a number of surprises, such as the discovery that magnets could only be obtained from the Guild of Conjurers, but no further delays.

"Hey, Tchornyo, let's race."

"Again? Mother's nose, Gardnyen, I'm sick of racing. That's all we ever do." It was a bright, windy day, and Tchornyo, recently reinstated at home after five dark weeks of disgrace, was feeling better than he'd felt since the murderous incident in the alley. Mother's Eye was beaming affectionately, Tchornyo's hair and beard were floating satisfactorily in the wind, and the last thing he wanted to do was darken the day with a dalber race.

"Hah! You're only sick of racing because you never win."

This was true, but Tchornyo felt called upon nevertheless to say, "What are you talking about? My Boustrophedon can beat your old Galimatias any day."

This assertion made a race inevitable. "Hoo!" hooted Gardnyen. "Prove it. Come on, line up."

With the mocking assistance of the other young nobles who were there in the dalber pasture just outside the city gates, Tchornyo and Gardnyen managed to line up their blooded dalbers. The beasts, as usual, failed to understand what was expected of them. Tchornyo's Boustrophedon was especially nervous, and could only be controlled by the ardent use of spurs and heated language, which amused the crowd and humiliated Tchornyo. Already the race was spoiling the day for him.

"What's your bet?" Gardnyen asked, smiling.

Honor required Tchornyo to demonstrate his nonexistent confidence with a wager, and his dalber's nervousness required that he do so in a hurry. "Twenty-five on Boustrophedon," he blurted. It was a miserable day.

"Twenty-five? What is this, a game for children? I'll put fifty on Galimatias. Do you want odds?"

"Oh . . . No. I'll see you." That no one in the crowd could be persuaded to bet on Boustrophedon did not add to Tchornyo's cheer.

Somebody chanted the familiar starting ritual. "By your Mother, by your Father, by the King—And—GO!"

At the shout, Galimatias took off like a frightened pterodactyloid, scurrying at top speed around the oval track so eagerly that all Gardnyen had to do was hold on. But the shout only served to complete Boustrophedon's confusion. The dalber stood rock-still and froze, and nothing Tchornyo could say or do was enough to persuade the animal to run. While Gardnyen and Galimatias sped easily around the track and the other nobles variously cheered and jeered, Tchornyo grew red-faced from trying to urge his dalber into action, and his sense of humiliation deepened. The beautiful day was becoming a nightmare, as usual. Tchornyo hated racing.

The arrival of Galimatias back at the starting line, however, finally unfroze Boustrophedon, and while the crowd laughed, the dalber carried poor Tchornyo halfway across the field and then froze again. Tchornyo had to dismount and, avoiding dalber chips only partially successfully, lead Boustrophedon back to the starting point. Tchornyo's humiliation was, as usual, complete. Not even paying off the wager and listening to Gardnyen's joshing could bother him anymore. He was, by emotional default, a good loser.

Tchornyo was noticeably silent on the ride back to the stables. He had lost points in the constant battle for prestige among his companions. It seemed to Tchornyo that his point rating stood at an all-time low. He meditated on methods of regaining stature.

"Don't be so glum," one of his friends said over the lunch table. "It was only a dalber race."

"It's not that," Tchornyo answered, which was true; it was not only that but the whole accumulation of miseries over the past weeks. "It's the conspiracy." A sudden and happy inspiration!

"The conspiracy?" His friend was suddenly all ears.

"I have information," Tchornyo chose his words carefully, "that there is an antinobility conspiracy right here in Lylldarg." He suddenly had several more interested listeners.

"You mean another peasant uprising like that one three hundred years ago?" one of them asked.

Another brandished a *kabnon* leg like an imaginary sword. "We'll beat 'em into the ground," he said. "We won't even leave any of 'em for Mother's Wrath."

Tchornyo consolidated his position. "Not peasants," he said in a starkly mysterious manner. "My information indicates that there are more powerful forces involved." He was beginning to feel comfortably important again. *This*, Mother be praised, was a game he could really play. "I cannot say any more than that right now," he finessed.

Gardnyen snorted. "He's talking about those two Mother-lorn commoners who killed Garlyn and Drebnyo last month while he ran away."

Tchornyo gave his friend a dirty look, but refused to acknowledge the implied insult. Instead he countered this threat to his position by saying, "That was only the beginning."

"You mean there's more?" one of the group asked.

"More and worse," Tchornyo said darkly. "Remember how I hunted for the killers afterward and couldn't find them?" Everybody nodded. "I even checked everyone who attended the prayer meetings, twice a day for six days." Everybody nodded again.

Tchornyo pressed his advantage. "Well, think about this for a minute: every commoner in Lyffdarg attended the prayer meetings. The Temple records prove it. And even so, we didn't catch the killers. Furthermore, an Embrace of Guards searched the city during every prayer meeting to make sure no commoners were hiding, and they didn't find the killers either. And yet the killers were in the city all the time."

There was a startled gasp. Even Gardnyen was impressed enough to ask, "How do you know that?"

"Well, partly because the city gates were locked and no one, killers or not, could get out, but mostly," Tchornyo paused before firing his biggest gun, "mostly because I've seen them in the city since."

Everyone spoke at once. "When? Where? What were they doing? Why didn't you catch them?" The questions rattled in the air while Tchornyo prepared his answer.

The questions faded into a silence that Tchornyo allowed to stretch to the breaking point. Then he said, "I saw them five weeks ago in Lame Dalber Street, near the market. I don't know what they were doing, but the moment they saw me, they ran away. I tried to catch them, but their organization stopped me."

"What do you mean, organization?" Gardnyen asked. His tone was no longer cynical.

"Just that," Tchornyo answered smugly. "While I was chasing the killers, somebody tried to stop me by throwing crockery at me, somebody else tried to stop me by strewing field melons in my way, and somebody else actually did stop me by running me down with a herd of wild dalbers. And if that isn't organization enough for you, consider this: as soon as the herd of dalbers was finished with me, one of Mother's Guards arrested me. *That,* my friend, takes organization."

There was no possible reply. Everyone sat gloomily still, even Tchornyo, who had managed, without noticing, to convince himself. Finally one of the young nobles voiced the question all of them were thinking. "What are we going to do?"

Secretly delighted with his promotion from humiliated loser to acknowledged leader, Tchornyo said, "This is my plan . . ."

"This is my plan," Smith was saying. "Now that we've invented this Mother-lorn telegraph, the first thing we have to do is string wires between Lyffdarg and some other city. Then—"

"Stop."

"What's wrong, Hurd?"

"You can't string those wires without Temple approval."

"As a matter of fact," Ansgar Sorenstein contributed, "you can't do anything on this Motherless planet without Temple approval."

"That's not quite true," Hurd said patriotically. "You only need approval for things that haven't been done before."

"Hurd, old son, we're not planning to do much of anything here that *has* been done before," John said. "How do we go about getting Temple approval?"

To be approved by the Temple, it turned out, any innovation had to satisfy three conditions. It had to be free from any taint of heresy; it had to be, in the broadest sense of the word, useful, and it had to be in public demand or fill an acknowledged need.

"The first thing we have to do," John said the next day, after thinking about the problem all night, "is hold a private demonstration of the telegraph here in the workshop. We'll invite a few merchants, some nobles, two or three high-ranking army officers, the Commander of Mother's Guards and as many priests as want to attend. As soon as they see the telegraph in action, they'll see its possibilities. That way we'll be able to prove its usefulness and create a demand for it in one smooth operation."

"That's fine," commented Ansgar Sorenstein. "Now all we have to do is prove the gadget's orthodoxy. How do we do that, mastermind?"

"Oh, that's simple," Hurd volunteered. "Hire a Temple lawyer. If the telegraph is at all possible, a good lawyer can prove that *The Book of Garth Gar-Muyen Garth* predicted it, which makes it orthodox by definition."

"You know, it's amazing how very much like Terra Lyff can be sometimes," Pindar Smith concluded.

"Father, sir." Although he'd been reinstated now for more than two weeks, Tchornyo was still being cautiously polite.

"Please, son, I'm trying to read." And what with the standard Lyffan literacy rate, the elder Hiirlte was finding the handwritten invitation something of a chore.

"But Daddy—"

"Now don't bother me, Tchornyo. This letter seems to be rather important. These Gar-Terrayen fellows claim to be able to talk softly over great distances. You know, a trick like that might come in handy now and then." One of the reasons the elder Hiirlte was a duke was that habit of his of realizing that certain tricks might, indeed, come in handy now and then.

"But I want to tell you about the conspiracy!" Tchornyo's whine contained only the worst elements of his speaking voice.

"Tchornyo! Go away. I'm not interested in your childish conspiracies. When will you learn not to bother me with these unimportant things?"

Tchornyo, defeated, walked slowly away. He'd hoped to talk his father into financing the anticonspiracy committee, but now he'd have to look harder for the money. He had no doubt that he'd find it. Already he'd had some mysterious offers from men who were willing to trade cash for anonymity.

The Grand Duke Hiirlte, on the other hand, rang for

his business manager. These Gar-Terrayen boys obviously had a good thing going for them, and he wanted part of it.

"Smith, Mother-crush it, get over here! This damn—I mean Mother-lorn gadget doesn't work!" John Harlen was sitting precariously balanced on a wooden chair leaning over the first working model of the telegraph.

"What do you mean it doesn't work?" Pindar Smith came over to the table and stared into the wooden frame and its coils of copper wire.

"I mean I push this Mother-lorn key down and the damn sounder doesn't click. That's what I mean it doesn't work."

"Oh, great." Pindar pushed tentatively at one of the coils. "The demonstration is supposed to start in half an hour. Our illustrious invited guests should start arriving any time now. Great! And *you* had to bust . . . oh, here it is." Smith poked at a connection. "Now try it."

Harlen pressed the key and the clicker said, "Clunk."

"Clunk?" Harlen asked.

"I had to use a ceramic resonator," Smith explained sheepishly. "Here, let me solder that connection tight."

According to age-old Lyffan custom, the guests began arriving half an hour after the stated demonstration time. No one had thought to warn the Terrans of this, of course, and by the time the first nobleman drove up in his four-dalber coach, every nerve in the workshop was stretched more thin than the hand-drawn copper wires that connected the parts of the telegraph.

Nor had anyone thought to warn the Terrans that all the guests would arrive on dalbers. Ansgar Sorenstein, being the man least essential to the demonstration, was the logical choice for the post of dalber watcher. By the time he had forty-five gronching beasts in his charge, he was as unnerved as the rest of the Special Detail, but his particular fear was that all the invited guests would accept the invitation. The forty-five hysterical dalbers that were driving him toward madness represented only half of the guest list.

If the street outside the workshop looked like a rodeo, the workshop itself looked like a state fair exhibit. If the street outside didn't look like a rodeo, there is no way to explain what the workshop did look like. Along one wall were the dismantled elements of a complete two-station telegraph system. Another wall was taken up with graphic portrayals of how the instrument worked, laboriously drawn and colored by the dalber-plagued Ansgar Sorenstein. At the back of the room, on a very small podium, Hurd explained the benefits of telegraphy in his most flawlessly poetic diction, while Pindar Smith at the front door sent messages along the wires to John Harlen at the back door. The first message said, "What hath Mother wrought?" which caused no little confusion among the guests.

"And how'd ye say the Mother-lorn message gets across these Mother-lorn little threads?" asked an army officer.

"Mother's Spirit, reverend lords, is dwelling in yon batteries. When that a message would be sent, our Mother hasteneth to speed it," Hurd answered gracefully.

"What'd the Mother-lorn blighter say?" the army officer asked John.

"Electricity in the batteries," John answered curtly. He was trying to decipher Smith's amateurish transmissions, and had no patience with technical questions.

"Ye don't say so," the officer mused to himself. Then, much more loudly, he said, "Look here, fellows, these Mother-lorn blighters 'ave got Mother 'erself workin' for 'em. They keep her in these Mother-lorn crocks over here."

"Ain't that blasphemy, Father?" someone asked one of the priests attending the demonstration.

"No, son," the priest responded gravely. "It sounds more like good politics to me."

Doctor Jellfte hung around in the background, lending the respectability of his title to the proceedings. Nobody noticed him more than enough to remark on his presence, which served to guarantee that this endeavor was not some fly-by-night outfit. Certainly, no one thought to ask him any questions, which was just as well.

All in all it was a successful demonstration. Nobody failed to see the telegraph's utility and value. Only one army officer was burned by battery acid, and he was not severely burned. The priests didn't seem to think there was anything heretical in the instrument, though, of course, they reserved comment, and possibly judgment, until the upcoming Temple trial. The only really sticky moment came after the demonstration was over.

After everyone had thanked everyone else for the demonstration and/or for being present at it, the guests still refused to go home. They hung around the door in embarrassed clumps, as though none was willing to leave before all the others had. Finally Spoln Gar-Tchornyen Hürlte, a very important nobleman, whispered to Pindar Smith, "I say, old man, where in Mother's Name have you hidden the *tray?*"

No one had told Pindar Smith anything about a tray. He tapped out a message to John. "Where is the tray?"

"Hurd," John asked, "do you know where the tray is?"

"What tray?" Hurd asked.

John tapped out a message to Smith. "What tray?"

Smith looked up from the key and asked the duke, "What tray, sir?"

"Why, the Mother-lorn tray for us to leave our cards in, of course. How else do you expect us to register our interest? That's what we're all waiting in this Mother-lorn doorway for, after all."

Smith relayed this information back to John, who related it to Hurd. "Mother's nose," Hurd said angrily. "How could I have forgotten?" He ran upstairs and returned with an ornate silver tray, which he set on a table near the front door. Then the guests filed out, most of them leaving their cards in the tray.

Tchornyo sat nervously at the back of the tavern. He had never had a secret appointment with anyone before, and he was sure that everyone else in the room was watching him. At the stroke of three, the appointed time, a short, well but plainly dressed man entered the tavern and walked directly to his table.

"You are Tchornyo Gar-Spolnyen Hiirlte?" the man asked.

Tchornyo stood up. "Yes sir. Would you care to join me?" The man dropped into a chair across the table. Tchornyo, looking nervously around, sat down.

"I am here," the stranger announced, "to speak for a man of high position who would prefer that his name not be brought into this, but who wishes to provide your organization with financial support in recognition of the important work you are liable to be doing. Is that clear?"

"Yes," said Tchornyo, who had recognized the words "financial support" very clearly.

"Fine. The operation will work as follows: we will give you every month a certain amount of money, based on the total number of members in your organization at the end of the previous month. You, in return, will supply us with a membership list and a report of all your activities."

". . . and he fell for it?"

"Like a *kabnon* in a corn patch." The mysterious little man was reporting to his superior. "Every time I said 'money' his eyes lit up. He didn't hear anything else. I managed to get through to him, after several repetitions, that the more members he recruited, the more money we'd give him. By the end of next month he'll have every noble son in Lyffdarg in his anticonspiracy committee. He'll make up beautiful reports to send us."

"Good." The high Lyffan noble rubbed his hands together. "He wants a conspiracy, does he? Wait a bit—we'll give him one!"

The Temple trial struck the Terrans as being more like a Sunday school lecture than a courtroom drama. Their lawyer stood up and read a series of scriptural quotations (from *The Book of Garth Gar-Muyen Garth*), then Doctor Jellfte, as the most noble member of the Gar-Terrayen clan, stood up and read a series of short paragraphs composed by Hurd that described the telegraph in what amounted to liturgical terms. Then the High Priest and Father of the Fathers, an extraordinarily noble Lyffan who had no other name, said, "The innovation satisfieth Scripture. Until it be proven either harmful or harmless, We extend to it Our conditional approval." Then prayers were said and everybody went home.

8

For everyone concerned, the first year was the hardest.

The Terrans, for example, were caught up in the intricacies of Lyffan finance. Having obtained ecclesiastical approval, they now had to form a company to exploit their invention. This was simple enough in essence, but some of the attendant formalities were complex beyond belief.

First of all, it was necessary to elevate one of the Terrans, most obviously Pindar Smith, to the nobility, so that the Gar-Terrayen clan could deal with other nobles on an equal basis. Doctor Jellfte's title, being appointive rather than acclamative, was not good enough, since it couldn't be inherited or otherwise dealt with according to the blood-linked traditions of Lyffan law. Thus Pindar Smith was made a baron.

Everyone who was interested in the telegraph attended Smith's elevation. Everyone, in this case, seemed to equal just about half the population of Lyffdarg. None of the younger nobles were present of course, they had their own interests to attend to, but all the older noblemen were gathered, along with representatives of the army and the clergy, in the great hall of King Osgard Gar-Osgardyen Osgard's palace.

From the high wooden rafters of the great hall hung the smoke-stained, faded banners of Lyff's great families. One banner stood out, mainly because it was fairly new, and therefore fairly bright. It bore the staff and twined serpents that, until that afternoon, had represented the clan Gar-Terrayen among the noble banners. Later, as part of the ceremonies, it would be removed, and a brand new banner, bearing a zigzag streak of silver like a flash of lightning, would take its place.

The elevation was preceded by a ninety-minute concert of archaic dodecaphonic music from what was sometimes called the golden age of Lyff. It was during this concert that Smith's nerves began to go back on him.

"I tell you, Doc, I can't do it," he protested in a heavy whisper to Doctor Jellfte, who had gone through this before.

"It's just the music that's bothering you, my boy," the older man replied with nostalgic patience. "I remember, it rather upset me, too. This ancient stuff takes getting used to."

"No, Doc, it's not the music. It's the whole idea. Becoming a nobleman and all that. I've never believed in that sort of thing, you know, and . . . well, I'm afraid I'll—"

"Sweet Mother, man, you're not going to be sick, are you?"

"No, Doc. I'm just afraid I'll forget my lines."

"Is that all that's bothering you? My word! Don't worry about your lines, Smith. Everyone forgets his lines. It's almost a tradition by now. Don't let *that* bother you. King Osgard's a very good-natured, progressive sort of chap, really. He won't mind if you forget your lines, he'll just fill in for you. Why, I forgot my own lines, I did, and he whispered every response to me, just like some Mother-lorn prompter."

Oddly enough, given that assurance Smith didn't forget his lines at all, and the three hour ceremony went off without a hitch, much to King Osgard's surprise.

The reception after the elevation was rather more complicated. No one had mentioned to Smith that he had to fight a duel with the highest ranking nobleman in order to establish the company.

"Damn it," he said, reverting to Terran notions in his excitement, "no one ever tells me anything. If I had known about this duel, I wouldn't have gone along with this scheme for a minute. I can't go out there and kill a nobleman with everybody watching and all. It's just not done."

"But you're not supposed to kill him," Hurd replied soothingly. "It's all just a ritual, just make-believe. In fact, he's supposed to kill you."

"Me? That's even more out of the question. I refuse to be killed."

"Not really killed, you Motherless dalberson. I told you, it's all make-believe. You're fighting with blunt, padded swords. You couldn't even bruise anybody with them. He represents the stockholders, understand? It's all symbolic."

It was all of that. Only symbolism could have explained that strange charade. The oldest imaginable nobleman, the eighty-three-year-old Duke Terdryo Gar-Gardnyen Tsolistran, aided and moderately abetted by two only slightly younger nobles, one on each side, approached Smith at something like one pace per minute, waved a thickly padded baton twice in the air over Smith's head, and then dropped the baton with the force of a butterfly's kiss on Smith's shoulder. Smith, well-prompted by Hurd, fell to the floor, saying, "I yield, sire. I yield."

Then old Duke Terdryo mouthed some incomprehensible phrases about, presumably, the company's duty to its stockholders, Smith agreed, and the Lyffan Telegraph Trust became a going concern.

"What we need," Gardnyen announced, "is a symbol." He had become Tchornyo's chief aide-de-camp and advisor, all of their old feuds having been forgotten in the new adventure. It is true that Tchornyo seldom took Gardnyen's advice, but then Tchornyo seldom took anyone's advice.

"A symbol? What sort of symbol do you mean?" Tchornyo asked. They were sitting in the office of their new headquarters building, which had been rented with the first installment of their secretive benefactor's largess.

"Some sort of distinguishing mark we could wear."

"But this is supposed to be a secret society."

"Oh I don't mean in public or on the street or anything like that, but we could wear it at meetings and when we drill and like that."

"But all members are checked at the door before they come in to a meeting—they don't have to wear anything to identify themselves."

"Oh Tchornyo, you don't know what I mean—forget it." The conversation lapsed into silence. Tchornyo went outside the office to look at the new recruits, who were just taking the oath. They were all standing in a line with their right hands clasped symbolically over their left hands at chest level in front of them.

"We swear," they were saying, "to be faithful to the Anti-Conspiracy Committee, and to obey without question the orders of our superiors in the Committee whatever such orders might be. We swear to be vigilant in our search for the conspirators wherever they may be found. In Mother's Sacred Name we swear this."

Tchornyo walked over to the Committeeman who had administered the oath after the ceremony. "How many do we have now?" he asked.

"With that batch—two hundred sixty-seven."

Tchornyo smiled. "Progress," he said. "Progress." He went back into the office. "You know," he said to Gardnyen, "that oath is a very good sounding thing. Only I wonder why that little man wanted it in just that form?"

Gardnyen couldn't figure it out either.

"Damn it all," Admiral Bellman said, "this thing is worse than space chess. At least with three-dimensional chess, I know how many men I've got and where they are."

"I'm sorry, Chief," said the young security officer who was the sole audience for Bellman's unhappiness. "I'm sorry," he repeated, "but we couldn't find a leak anywhere."

"Damn it all, man," the Admiral shouted, unmindful of noise or redundancy, "there *has* to be a leak. How else did Senator Walsh find out about the Special Detail?"

Meanwhile, Senator Walsh was chortling happily over a slip of paper that had been delivered to him with his breakfast. "Very interesting," he said, chuckling. "Yes indeed, very interesting." Then he raised his voice and said, "Gordon."

"Yes sir," answered the valet.

"Gordon," the senator said more softly, "will you please look something up for me in the *Encyclopedia Galactica?* See what the book says about a planet called Lyff. L-y-f-f. That's a good man."

As Gordon left to check the encyclopedia, Senator Walsh resumed his happy chortling.

"Nonsense," Admiral Bellman raged on. "That old fogey couldn't possibly have guessed all those details. I tell you, we have a Consie spy in our midst. Now get out and find him."

Shaking his head wearily, the young officer left Bellman's office and gave orders for the third consecutive mass interrogation of the whole headquarters company. Bellman and his security leaks! Why, the very idea was insulting.

"Yes," said Tchornyo proudly, "we now have more than six hundred members."

"Splendid," the well-dressed little stranger said. "My employer will be most heartened by your progress."

"I think six hundred members in two months is very good," Gardnyen added needlessly.

"That's what I said," the small man snapped. "Here." He handed a leather bag, obviously full of money, to Tchornyo. "This should take care of you for a while. Now I want to examine the premises."

"You mean you want us to show you around?" Tchornyo asked, at the same time emptying the bag out on the table and beginning to count the heavy gold coins.

"No," said the stranger, "I want to examine the premises. I can show myself around quite well, thank you."

"But sir, much of what goes on here is secret," Gardnyen insisted.

The stranger sneered. "So, young man, is all that," gesturing toward the money on the table. Then he left the office and started to inspect the building.

"I don't like this at all," Gardnyen whispered to Tchornyo.

"Why not? It doesn't seem to be counterfeit, does it?"

"No, you dalberson idiot, not the money. *Him.*"

"Him?"

"Him. Who does he represent? Where is all this money coming from? I think we should know more about this. After all, he may well be part of . . . you know . . . of the conspiracy."

"You're crazy," Tchornyo explained simply.

Nevertheless, when the stranger left the building, Tchornyo and Gardnyen unobtrusively followed him. Though he did not seem to notice he was being followed, the stranger led Tchornyo and Gardnyen a long and twisting chase through the ill-lit older quarter of Lyffdarg. If it hadn't been for the emptiness of the streets, the young noblemen might easily have lost sight of their quarry several times. Finally, Tchornyo grew tired of walking.

"If we walk a little faster," he said to Gardnyen, "we might be able to follow him more easily."

"So what? We're following him easily enough, aren't we?"

"That all depends. Where *is* he?"

The stranger was gone. Since there were no convenient corners for him to have ducked around, it seemed logical to assume he'd entered one of the low, narrow buildings that lined the twisting street like ill-made bricks, but which building it was impossible to tell.

"Blast!" said Gardnyen. "Where is he?"

"Forget him. What I want to know is, where are we?"

"I don't know. I've never been in this neighborhood before."

"Psst," hissed a voice from the shadows. "You boys want a little sister?"

"Well," said Gardnyen, "that settles where we are. Now how do we get back home?"

How they got back home was very slowly. Lyffdarg's red-light district was unusually extensive and amazingly like a maze, almost as though it had been designed especially to confuse such wanderers as Tchornyo and Gardnyen. It was not until they discovered that they were near the Temple that they had any chance of finding their way home at all, and even then the task took several hours.

A high Lyffan noble rubbed his hands together in politely controlled glee. "So they tried to follow you, eh? Funny."

"Yes," the mysterious little man agreed. "They were as furtive as dalbers in rut, sir. It was almost a sin to confuse them further, but I finally grew weary of playing with them."

"Hah. And where did you leave them?"

"In the Street of Many Flowers, three blocks from here."

"That was most considerate of you. The little sisters will no doubt help the boys get home again."

"I hope so," said the little man. Then he made his report to his superior. It was a most satisfactory report.

John Harlen paced up and down the telegraph office furiously. He was yelling and gesturing wildly at the operations manager, who was staring unhappily at the floor. "By Mother's eyes man, that makes the twenty-seventh time in only six months of operation. What's happening out there?"

The manager sighed and shifted his gaze to the ceiling. "We don't know any more than we report."

"You don't report anything useful. Here, look." He waved the report in front of the manager's nose. "Service on the line from Lyffdarg to Prymilbos—which incidently is our only line—has been temporarily discontinued due to a break in the line." He snorted. "And when you go out to find the break—have you?" The manager nodded. "You'll find that two of the poles have been knocked down and the wire taken. Is the report back yet?" The manager nodded again. "Isn't that what happened?" The manager shifted his gaze back to the floor and nodded again. John stopped pacing and looked determined. "I think it's about time that I took a look at one of these breaks. How far away is this one?"

"About twelve sterbs."

John grabbed his square hat decorated with a large feather, standard attire in Lyffdarg, and perched it at a ridiculous angle on his head. "Come with me Prudyo, I'm going to examine this one myself."

Later, John described the scene to his partners. "Bandits, they say," he said furiously, stalking up and down the long workshop like a detective on a scent. "Bandits. They knock down two poles with dynamite—dynamite, mind you, and as far as we knew dynamite hadn't even been invented yet—knock down two poles, remove the wire and vanish."

"How did bandits get hold of dynamite?" Sorenstein inquired.

"The question is, who made the dynamite for them to get hold of?" John amended.

"A better question," said Hurd, "is why do the bandits want copper wire?"

"I know where they got the dynamite," Pindar Smith volunteered. The rest of the group turned toward him and waited for an explanation.

"You see," Smith said when the silence had made clear what everyone wanted, "we needed dynamite to dig holes for some of those Mother-lorn poles—that desert rock is hard—so I invented dynamite."

"Gee, Pin," John said gently, "I wish you had told me."

"It slipped my mind."

"Great, Pin, just great. And where did the bandits get hold of dynamite?"

"Oh, that. Well, you told us that we should hire as many native subcontractors as possible—"

"That's right. Spread the new techniques around. So?"

"So I hired the Guild of Pharmacists to make dynamite for us."

"And it never crossed your mind that the Guild of Pharmacists might sell the stuff to somebody else?"

"Well . . . no. I didn't think about that."

"That's all right, Pin. But did you stop, perhaps, to think that dynamite can also be used as a weapon?"

"Weapon? Oh, I see what you mean. No, I didn't think about that, either."

"Great. Hurd, what do you know about these bandits?"

"They call themselves the People's Army. They're a sort of revolutionary party, antinobles, anticlergy, they're even against the King, some of them."

"That's what I thought. And now they have dynamite. That's just the sort of blunder that leads to cultural disruption. The last thing we want is to have all our work undone by an unplanned revolution."

Just then an acolyte of the Guild of Proclaimers entered the workshop. "Your pardon, noble sires," he said. Then he cleared his throat and proclaimed at the top of his voice, "To the Members and Officers of the Lyffan Telegraphic Trust, greetings and blessings. The High Priest and Father of the Fathers, may Mother cherish his name, requests that you show cause why the operations of the Lyffan Telegraphic Trust should not be suspended and its Temple charter should not be summarily revoked. The High Priest and Father of the Fathers, may Mother cherish his name, requests that such cause be shown on or before Mother's Day of the present month. In Mother's Secret Name, so be it spoken." Whereupon the acolyte left, without waiting for questions or comment.

"Now what the hell is all *that* about?" John raged.

It was mostly about the Guild of Guilds.

"You must understand, dear sir," the High Priest told John the next day, "that we of the Temple have no objections to your telegraph. Indeed, we are most appreciative of its uses, and if you are forced to surrender your charter, we intend to carry your work forward ourselves. No, it is not the Temple that brings this cause against you, but rather the Guild of Guilds."

"I see, sir," said John respectfully. This was his first encounter with the Temple, and he was less than sure of himself. In such a case, he knew, respect is often as useful as wisdom. "What is the Guild of Guilds' complaint?"

The High Priest ranked second only to the King in nobility. This, of course, made him easier to deal with than most of the Lyffan upper class. Not having to worry about position and security, he was free to direct his attention to more, perhaps, trivial, but certainly more interesting, affairs. "Their major complaint," he said, "is that you people are not a guild. They have noticed—as who has not?—that you are making a great deal of money, and they want some of it. That is what lies behind their stated objections, which are mainly that you are taking work away from established guilds, particularly the Guild of Scribes and the Guild of Messengers, and that your schools are infringing on the rights of the Temple. Both of these objections will be answered by your forming a guild and joining the Guild of Guilds, which is what I recommend. Of course, you must tell no one that I have given you this suggestion."

"Certainly, your grace," said John. After polite conversation, a glass of wine, and the High Priest's formal blessing, John Harlen went home to organize a guild.

Osgard Gar-Osgardnyen Osgard, King and Father of Lyff, was, as has been mentioned, a most good-natured and progressive gentleman. He was also a most astute politician and businessman. Therefore John decided to accept Doctor Jellfte's advice and tell the king everything.

"Fantastic," the king said. "Oh, not that I don't believe you, you understand, but you must admit it *is* fantastic." John agreed with him. "But if we only have ten—no, nine now—years in which to learn how to defend ourselves against these mysterious invaders, why doesn't your—um —planet send in a large number of people and get the whole thing over with quickly instead of being so sneaky about it?"

John explained to King Osgard that the Consie Party back on Terra would yell like a stricken dalber if it found out about the mission at all. This led into an explanation of Terran politics which fascinated the king and lasted for a good half-hour.

After a few more questions the king agreed to sponsor the proposed Guild of Telegraphers. "This isn't exactly altruism on my part, you know," he explained, "nor is it due completely to the story you have told me. You must realize that your invention is a very good thing from my point of view. Not only does your Telegraph Trust pay a good stiff tax, but my commanders report that they find the instrument very useful in a military way."

The king himself escorted the Terrans to a side entrance to the palace. "To escape that throng out front," he explained. "Well, if there's anything else I can do for you people just let me know. And don't worry, I'll take your advice and not tell anyone else about this. Who would believe me?"

9

The Anti-Conspiracy Committee was almost a year old, and had more than five thousand members. The first Committee project was in full swing, and every day from dawn to dawn squads of Committeemen patrolled the streets of Lyffdarg, hunting for conspirators.

Sooner or later one of these patrols was bound to meet and recognize Hurd and John, though Tchornyo's rather fanciful description of the killers eased somewhat the dangers of recognition. As it happened, this encounter took place when John and Hurd left the palace after enlisting the aid of King Osgard, and the squad of Committeemen they met was led, alas, by Tchornyo himself.

"There they are!" Tchornyo shouted. Since discipline was not the Committee's strongest point, this caused some confusion, just enough to give John and Hurd a head start.

"There who are?" asked Gardnyen.

"The killers, you dalberson, the killers! There they are!"

"Where?" asked somebody else.

"Right over there, you fools. Catch them!"

John and Hurd turned a corner and started running. Before they had gone ten paces, they heard the Committeemen charging down on them like a herd of gronching dalbers.

"This way," shouted a voice that was probably Tchornyo's.

"Sweet Mother of Everything," John whispered. "I suspect we've had it."

75

"Not yet," Hurd whispered back. "Follow me."

It was a narrow, dark, twisting, and much intersected street. Indeed, the whole neighborhood, one of the oldest in the city, was built more or less along the lines of a labyrinth. Hurd knew the area intimately from his recent career as a criminal.

As John and Hurd turned a corner, they heard a sharp explosion and a sustained twanging noise. "Those people have guns," John said quietly.

"Guns?"

"Yes. We were going to invent them for our telegraph police, but someone seems to have beaten us to the punch. Smith and his damned dynamite. Are you sure you know where we're going?"

"Of course I am. I have friends around here."

The chase was getting louder, and lights were going on in windows along the way.

"There they are," Tchornyo shouted. Two shots rang out, and many of the lights along the way went nervously out again. No one in that neighborhood wanted to borrow trouble.

Hurd and John turned another corner, then ran up an alley, climbed a fence, and emerged on another street. "That should take care of our noisy friends," Hurd said happily. "Now let's see if Sister Panja can sneak us home."

"Who is Sister Panja?" They were walking fairly slowly down a street that looked exactly like the street from which they'd just escaped. All streets in that quarter looked alike.

"She's one of the little sisters," Hurd explained. "She doesn't work much anymore because she's growing old, but she knows everything there is to know about this part of Lyffdarg. She's very influential around here, too. She can even influence Mother's Guards, which is awfully important in a red-light district. Anyway, she lives right around the corner here— Oooph!"

Hurd managed, in turning the corner, to run into and

knock down Tchornyo, who was leading half his squad of Committeemen in a house to house search.

"Gyaah!" Tchornyo screamed. "They're here! The killers!"

The three members of the squad leaped on John and Hurd valiantly, swinging and slugging and hitting them almost as often as they hit each other. Tchornyo got to his feet and stood in the middle of the street blowing what must have been signals on what might have been a bugle. All the lights in the neighborhood went on, faces appeared at all the lighted windows, and all the lights went off again almost at once. It was that kind of neighborhood.

The Committeemen had much to learn about street fighting, and John and Hurd were ideal teachers. Before Tchornyo had finished his first bugle fantasia, John had taught someone not to strike from above. The student lay groaning on the filthy cobblestones while the battle raged around him.

"Assassins!" Tchornyo shrieked improbably. "Help!" Then he started another bugle selection.

Acting in tandem, John and Hurd managed to convince another Committeeman that knives are not polite. This student didn't groan. He was far too busy bleeding. The third Committeeman, seeing how expensively his friends had learned their lessons, turned and ran for help. Instead of taking care of Tchornyo, which they certainly should have done, John and Hurd ran off in the other direction. Tchornyo continued to play his bugle.

Before they had gone half a block, Hurd and John heard shots again. "Those boys don't waste much time," John panted. Hurd had no breath to spare to answer him.

They turned corners blindly, two right turns and a left, two rights and a left, zigzagging through the city's ripest slum. The Committeemen were never more than half a block behind them, egged on by Tchornyo's impossible trumpeting.

No neighborhood, not even the most disreputable and

timid, could long pretend indifference to this rackety chase. If Tchornyo's bugle calls didn't serve to bring the neighbors to the streets, the Committeemen's shots—the first the city had ever heard—certainly did. The streets were growing dangerously crowded.

John and Hurd turned another corner, onto a wider, more brightly lighted street. Seconds later the Committeemen turned the corner, stopped, and puzzledly surveyed the empty thoroughfare.

"Follow me," a soft and somewhat grainy voice whispered. The darkness was enormous. Almost, John could feel it flexing its muscles.

"Come on," Hurd whispered.

They seemed to be in a long hallway or tunnel with hay strewn on the stone floor. They had ducked into the first open door they saw after turning the corner, without giving themselves time to identify the building. John was less than happy with the situation, but Hurd, more versed in the ways of the underworld, was content to follow the sandy voice blindly.

As they walked on and John's eyes adjusted to the new conditions, the darkness seemed, impossibly, to deepen. The wider John's pupils became and the more light they were prepared to admit, the more heavily conscious John became of the fact that in this place there was no light at all. Thus, after they had been walking for fifteen minutes, when their guide stopped and threw open a door, the light that streamed into the long hall blinded John, even though it was produced by nothing more brilliant than one cheap and smoky candle.

Their guide turned out to be a young woman. "Here they be, Mother," she said. "Yon bully boys was nearly on 'em when I opened up the door."

From within the room a silvery voice asked, "Did anybody see you take them in?"

"No, mum," the girl replied. "I peeked up the street and down, mum, and they wasn't no one looking."

"Very good, my dear. You may go to bed now." The silvery voice ran up and down the scale like a young melody trying its legs. "Won't you step inside a minute, boys?"

The owner of this lovely voice was the most grossly fat woman John had ever seen. She lay, amoeboid, sprawled on an ancient couch from which she obviously could not rise unaided, and except for the small, hidden motion of her jaw when she spoke and the constant darting of her eyes back and forth, back and forth, she was utterly motionless. "Don't let it frighten you," she chimed. "I used to be as pretty as any little sister, back when I was a girl. You'll get used to me."

Hurd knew what to do. "Good evening, Mother," he said courteously. "My name is Hurd, and this is my friend, John."

"You needn't call me Mother, boy. I just make the girls do that. It keeps them under control. I hear you've got yourselves a problem out there." There was, of course, no answer to that, and she talked on without waiting for one.

"Little Lord Tchornyo and his friends are very stubborn. They only have one idea, and they're not even sure what it is. Very dangerous. But don't you worry, boys, we'll save you."

This was a bit too much for John. "Great," he said, "but just who are you?"

"We're Mother's Little Helpers," the woman said, trying horribly to smile.

Tchornyo was almost helpless from the glory of it all. Now everybody in Lyff knew about the conspiracy, his committee was suddenly an element of great importance in Lyffan life, and he, Tchornyo Gar-Spolnyen Hiirlte, was a national hero. It was almost too much to believe. His most megalomaniacal dreams had never equaled this reality. He even had an honorary commission in Mother's Guards.

Most important to him, though, was the fact that everybody believed in the conspiracy, that he was no longer a laughingstock, that the menace that had been no more than a joke when only he feared it was now the common terror. His dedication to the capture and destruction of the killers resembled a religious frenzy.

His pride in self and position would have suffered had he realized that he himself was responsible for the escape of the killers from the city. But on the day John and Hurd left Lyffdarg, Tchornyo was standing inspection duty at the main gate, and it was only on Tchornyo's personal okay that they managed to get out.

This was not because of any real carelessness on Tchornyo's part. He thought he was okaying the passes of Mother Balnya and two little sisters bound for the Temple in Prymilbos.

Twenty-five sterbs out of town the carriage stopped. "This is where you boys get out," said the bloated madam.

There was a small crowd waiting for them, mostly rough-dressed men who might have been farmers, plus a few equally rough-dressed men who could never by any stretch of the imagination be thought of as farmers. "The People's Army," the fat woman said with a pride that quite overrode both her usual cynicism and the group's shabby appearance.

John and Hurd, awkward in the women's clothing they were wearing, dismounted from the carriage.

"Hey, Mother Balnya," one of the waiting men shouted, "what kind of soldiers are these? We don't need little sisters out here."

"Laugh all you want," she shouted back. "These girls are the sharpest soldiers *you'll* ever see."

The loud, coarse laughter embarrassed Hurd almost as much as the courtesan's clothing he was wrapped in, but John refused to be ruffled by so healthy a thing as free laughter. No, it took one thing more to disturb him.

"Thank you, Mother Balnya," he said quietly, using

the laughter to provide him with polite privacy. "I'll try to repay your kindness as soon as I get back to the city."

There was an alien-to-her sympathy in her voice when she answered him. "Didn't anybody tell you?" she asked. "Why, boy, you can never come back to the city. The People's Army won't let you, and it wouldn't be safe. You'd best remember that. No matter what else happens, you can't come back."

Then the carriage turned around and drove in a cloud of hot summer dust back to Lyffdarg. At last John Harlen was disturbed.

10

The main difficulty in artificially accelerating the development of a culture is that there is no way to predict with any accuracy how large a part in this process the culture itself is likely to take. The unexpected uses to which the Lyffans put gunpowder, a mere incidental element in the Special Detail's first project, demonstrated this. A week after Pindar Smith engaged the Guild of Pharmacists to manufacture dynamite for the telegraph, some nameless Lyffan genius had invented gunpowder and firearms, and three weeks after that the Guild of Armorers was selling revolvers that would have been accepted gladly on the mythical American frontier. A year later the Guild of Gunsmiths was formed, much to the Special Detail's alarm, gunsmithry being an art the Detail had planned to introduce much later in Lyff's reformation.

A year after its formation, the Guild of Gunsmiths conducted, and then abandoned, experiments in rocket-powered flight, but the Special Detail slept better for never hearing about those experiments.

Instead of being the manipulative agent the Special Detail considered itself, it was really more of an agent of ferment. What it caused on Lyff was not so much a process as an explosion, an incredible and independent flowering of technology as surprising and inevitable as the sudden flowering of crystals in a supersaturated solution, and while they imagined they were in complete control of a process, the explosion swept them along as violently as it swept the planet Lyff.

Ansgar Sorenstein, for example, followed a rigorously

logical path of development from the hand-powered generator originally designed to recharge telegraph batteries, through a simple steam-powered generator, to the steam engine, but when he went forth to introduce his steam engine to Lyff, he found that a few nobles were already riding around in steam-powered automobiles. Some Lyffan metalworker had already and independently drawn an equally logical but more subtle inference from the fact that the generator used wheels.

In the four years that followed the disappearance of John and Hurd, the workshop on Lame Dalber Street became an important center of research and technology, but it did not become, as it had been expected to, the only or even the most important such center.

Lyff had been waiting a thousand years for the impetus the Special Detail provided, but when that impetus was finally given, Lyffan development followed Lyffan lines. The Guild of Jewelers invented transistors only a few months after the Guild of Telegraphers introduced vacuum tubes. And before that, Lyffan philosophers, reasoning from the fact of electricity, had laid down a logical basis for the science of electronics.

The Terrans did, indeed, spark a revolution, but it was a Lyffan revolution. This, of course, was just as it should have been, but the feeling of being not quite in control of a process they had initiated combined with their uneasiness over the continued absence of John Harlen and Hurd Gar-Olnyn Saarlip to give the members of the Special Detail restless nights and uncomfortable dreams.

If the projects of the Special Detail flourished in an awkward manner, the affairs of the Anti-Conspiracy Committee throve in a manner most satisfactory and comfortable to Tchornyo Gar-Spolnyen Hiirlte and his mysterious backer. In a mere four years, membership in the Committee rose from a mere few hundred to more than ten thousand. Branches were established in all the major cities of Lyff. A special division that was established for commoners soon became the largest force in the movement, and Tchornyo himself became an important political figure.

The Committee grew to represent the conservative element in Lyffan thinking, a political party, in effect, as powerful on Lyff as the Consies were on Terra. There were, of course, no elections for the Committee to sway, but more and more governmental and religious decisions came to be based on the idea of keeping the Committee happy. High-ranking Lyffans were in fact and custom immune to the forces of popular opinion, but they were not immune to force *per se,* and since the Anti-Conspiracy Committee was in effect a private army, it represented the constant possibility of rebellion, a possibility that had never existed before Tchornyo's inspiration after the race, and a possibility that never once crossed Tchornyo's mind. He was far too happy with his power ever to dream of using it.

How the mysterious backer felt about the Committee's success during those four years is, of course, difficult to determine. He most likely approved, for every man delights in the prosperity of his enterprises. We may take the fact that during these four years he remained the Committee's major source of income as a sign of his approval.

That he chose to remain in the background all this time is another sure sign that he approved of the Committee's progress. He had, after all, ends of his own in mind when he endowed the Committee, and if Tchornyo's organization had ever threatened those ends, we may be sure that this nameless benefactor would have instantly reformed the Committee and destroyed the threat.

For all its noble patriotism, however, the Anti-Conspiracy Committee was responsible for the first real threat to the Lyffan way of life to arise in three hundred years. The Committee was not content to search for conspirators, it also managed to capture conspirators, and thus to create the very conspiracy it was dedicated to stamping out. The Committee conducted a continual inquisition, a continual witch hunt, and found conspirators everywhere. If a man complained about taxes, a commoner, that is, he was automatically arrested and tried as a conspirator, and whether he was convicted or acquitted, his arrest made real conspirators of his friends and himself. Everywhere the Committee discovered conspiracy, conspiracy promptly took root and flourished.

The ranks of the People's Army grew daily. For every man the Committee arrested, five disgruntled Lyffans joined the rebels. Soon it was no longer possible to dismiss the People's Army as a pack of bandits. Telegraph lines were sabotaged, villages were raided, priests were kidnaped, the number of outrages perpetrated by the rebels grew almost as rapidly as the number of arrests made by the Committee. The commoners were perfectly willing to put up with the dictatorship they'd always known, but they refused to put up with the new tyranny of the Committee.

Pitched battles between units of the People's Army and units of the Committee became so commonplace that they hardly rated mention in the newspaper Pindar Smith started as soon as the Lyffan Telegraph Trust was firmly established. And the rebels won every battle. No matter what new technical developments the Committee was able to bring to bear against them, the rebels remained constantly one development ahead of the Committee.

This, more than anything else in their confusing assignment, disturbed the members of the Special Detail. They could not escape the conclusion that the greatest force for progress on the planet was completely out of their hands, that Lyffan technology was developing along lines that were not only beyond their control, but also beyond their knowledge. There was no way to anticipate what new weapons the rebels were likely to use in any given battle, no way to tell what technological groundwork preceded each new weapon, and, worst of all, no guarantee that the rebels might not actually outstrip the Terrans and destroy Lyff before the Special Detail was able to finish saving it.

Nevertheless, the Terrans felt confident enough to celebrate the fifth anniversary of their arrival on Lyff with a magnificent party at the workshop. None of the guests, with the known exception of King Osgard, had any idea why the Gar-Terrayen boys were giving the party, but they all accepted the invitation to attend, partly because the Gar-Terrayens were very important people, but mostly because a party is, after all, a party.

The anniversary celebration was the most brilliant social event of the season. Not only King Osgard, but almost all the most highly placed nobles attended, as well as the entire upper level of the Temple hierarchy and the Board of Governors of the Guild of Guilds. The workshop glittered with rich clothing, and the new electric lights, still a novelty, multiplied the glitter until Ansgar Sorenstein was heard to wish he'd brought along his sunglasses.

There were fine wines and exotic foods, brought at great expense from the most distant provinces of Lyff, thanks to the Guild of Metal Workers' experimental fleet of steam-powered trucks. The entertainment ranged from the inevitable recital of ancient chamber music to erotic dances by the youngest and most attractive little sisters available.

At the height of the celebration, Pindar Smith made a speech. "Through the years," he said in part, "the Lyffan Telegraphic Trust has been intimately associated with the technical revolution that is transforming Lyff before our very eyes. The Trust's inventions have made life more interesting and yet more comfortable for every Lyffan, the Trust's schools have made illiteracy and rank superstition things of the past, the Trust's philosophy has changed Lyff from a kingdom to a planet, and the Trust's example has made experiment and invention the general preoccupation of the Lyffan people. Tonight, as we have often done before, we are going to introduce a new invention to Lyff, but tonight, for the first time, we are going to introduce not one of our own inventions, but something that was created by one of our employees, a man who, five years ago, could neither read nor write, had never had an independent idea, and had no hope for any future that was not a mere repetition of the past. Mother, in blessing the Trust, has blessed all of Lyff, and as a proof of this, it gives us great pleasure to present the invention of Tolnye Gar-Pferdnyan Soltchi, a cobbler's son. We call this invention the radio."

The guests, well-trained by previous demonstrations, applauded wildly as a red curtain was drawn back to disclose Lyff's first radio, a bulky thing that, at first glance, showed more signs of Lyff's well-developed tradition of cabinet-making than of the planet's new technology.

"With this instrument," Smith continued, "we can communicate over vast distances as rapidly as we can speak. We are no longer limited to the time-consuming and difficult-to-learn processes of the telegraph and the teletype. Now we can talk to people in Prymilbos as easily as we talk to each other. A whole concept of distance has been abolished.

"As you leave this evening, you will be given a pamphlet that explains how the radio works. Therefore, instead of explaining tonight, I will only demonstrate. This cabinet is what we call a receiver, this box on top of it is what we call a transmitter, and this thing in my hand is what we call a microphone. We have placed a similar receiver, transmitter, and microphone in the telegraph office in Astindarg, nine hundred sterbs away from here in the midst of the Northern Mountains.

"I'll speak into this microphone, the transmitter will send my voice nine hundred sterbs away to the receiver in Astindarg, where I will be heard by our local agent and the priest in charge of the Astindarg Temple. Then they will speak into their microphone, and we will hear them through this receiver. And all of this will take place as rapidly as we can talk, completely without delay."

While a breathless hush fell over the assembled guests, Smith spoke into the microphone. "Hello there," he said, "this is Lyffdarg calling Astindarg. Come in, Astindarg."

And from the receiver came a high-pitched, frightened voice, saying, "Help! Send troops! A space ship has just landed and the whole town is burning. Help! For Mother's sake, send. . . ." And then the voice died away and nothing could be heard but a steady hissing sound.

11

"No matter what else happens, you can't come back," the fat woman said. Then the carriage turned around and drove in a cloud of hot summer dust back to Lyffdarg.

John turned around and addressed the man who looked like the leader of the shabbily dressed group. "What did she mean, I can't go back to the city?"

The man laughed. "Why man, you're enlisting in the People's Army," he said. "The term of enlistment is six years, just like in the King's Army or Mother's Guards. Didn't you know?" From the way the man was laughing it seemed that his question was purely rhetorical.

One of the group came over to John and stood in front of him, with his arms on his hips. "Hey little girl, want to wrestle?" This question was not rhetorical. The man tried to grab John in a bear hug and John reacted automatically. The man found himself on the hard-packed ground. He got up and lunged at John . . . and found himself on the ground again. John was starting to enjoy himself. The man got up more slowly this time and started circling John. John made no move to attack, but just kept turning slowly to keep the man in front of him. Finally the man spat on the ground and grabbed for John's arm. He found himself on the ground again, but this time John was on top of him rubbing his face into the dirt.

"Have we wrestled?" John asked, letting the man up enough to answer.

"Yes," the man admitted.

"And tell me, who won?"

"You did, truly you did," the man said, as John applied a little more pressure to his arm. The whole group had gathered in a tight circle around the two to watch, and they were all looking very startled, all except Hurd. Hurd turned to the man closest to him and said, in a very low voice, "Boo." The man jumped.

"Alright now, enough playing," the man that John had picked out as the leader said. "You two have to be sworn into the People's Army. As an officer in the Army, I am authorized to administer the oath. Are you ready for it?"

John and Hurd went into a huddle. From the attitude of the group they decided that it would be more expedient to join the Army. They could always escape later and make their way back to the city. They took the oath, which was short and simple.

"Do you swear in Mother's Hidden Name to be loyal to the People's Army and, therefore, to the interests of the people?" asked the officer. They did so swear.

Dalbers were produced out of a nearby clump of trees, and John and Hurd rode off into the wilderness surrounded by their new comrades. After they had been riding for a few hours the officer rode alongside John and started talking to him.

"That seems to be a new style of wrestling you were using. I've never seen anything quite like it before." John admitted that it was uncommon in that part of Lyff. "I think," the officer said, "that the best use we could make of you would be to have you train the men in its use. I'm going to make a suggestion to that effect to the general."

John became interested. "The general? And who is the general?"

"You'll be meeting him in a few days. He'll answer all your questions himself." They rode on in silence.

Four days later they came to what looked like a small town hidden between two rocky gorges in the mountains. Sentries on rocks overlooking the narrow trail waved the group into the settlement.

"This," the officer announced, "is the headquarters of

the People's Army. I'll see whether the general wants to interview you now." They dismounted and the dalbers were led away.

John and Hurd, surrounded by their escort, waited uncomfortably in the middle of the street while the officer went off to check.

The officer was back within five minutes. "Follow me," he said, and set off again at a dog-trot. "We don't want to keep the general waiting," he yelled over his shoulder. John and Hurd obediently dog-trotted behind him.

The officer went in a door down the street and stopped in front of a desk, where he drew himself up to attention and saluted. "Two new men to see the general," he snapped. "He's expecting them."

The man behind the desk returned the salute casually. "Go right in," he said, waving toward a door behind him. The three of them went into the inner office.

General Garth, he called himself, omitting both clan and family names. This was part of his rebellion. And it wasn't even certain that Garth actually was his name. The common opinion in the People's Army was that he had adopted the name of Garth Gar-Muyen Garth, the founder of the Lyffan religion, to symbolize that his rebellion was not against the traditional social order but against abuses of that order. Naturally, no one dared ask him about this, and he didn't feel called upon to make explanations.

"The captain tells me you have a new way of wrestling," he said when John, Hurd, and the captain entered his office.

"Yes sir," John answered. "I call it 'judo.'"

"Judo," the general mused.

While General Garth mused, John observed. He liked what he saw. The old soldier was tall and lean, and gave the impression of great strength carefully controlled. His grey hair seemed to indicate wisdom more than it did age, and his eyes, which were as grey as his hair, indicated the kind of firmness a successful rebel must practice almost as a habit.

"You're John Garr-Terrayen Harlen." It was not a question.

"Yes sir," John said.

"Hmm. Any relation to the Gar-Terrayen clan that invented this new telegraph gadget?"

John admitted that he was one of those Gar-Terrayens, and explained his hypothetical position in the clan.

"I see. And what about this other fellow, Hurd Gar-Olnyn Saarlip?"

"He's my assistant," John explained. "In fact, you might almost call him my aide."

"Your aide, eh? Well, considering who you are and all, I think we owe you more of an explanation than you've had so far. With any luck at all, you should be very useful to us, but not if you don't know what's going on."

John insisted, rather too fulsomely, that his major ambition now was to serve the People's Army. The general then gave John's declaration the short thanks it deserved and launched into his explanation.

"To the rest of the world," he said, "we are only bandits. This is exactly what we want the rest of the world to think, which is the main reason we can't let you people return to Lyffdarg. In reality, we are a cleansing army, and when we are ready we will purge Lyff of the corruptions that are poisoning our people."

He talked for almost fifteen minutes, explaining and defending his desire to return Lyff to the healthy simplicity in which it began. "Lyff is giving up her strength in an orgy of decadence," he insisted. "More and more the comfort of the nobility and the clergy is assuming the importance our forefathers attached to the well-being of the people. Instead of being the protectors of the people Mother's law requires them to be, the nobles have become slave owners. And in thus blasphemously sapping the strength of the people, they are weakening themselves, and the whole nation with them."

John listened with delighted interest. This man, he realized, could, if his revolution succeeded, accomplish in two or three years what the Special Detail hoped to accomplish in ten. General Garth was the first real popular leader John had encountered on Lyff, and his support could mean the difference between failure and success for the Special Detail's mission.

"You're right, of course," John said when the general had finished his speech. "I'd never thought about it like that before, but you're obviously right. Mother knows, there's no real strength left in Lyffdarg."

"That's not true," General Garth insisted hotly. "There's as much strength in Lyffdarg as there always was, and it's in just the same part of Lyffdarg as it always was: the people. We don't want to bring strength to the city; we want to rouse the strength that's already there. That's the most important part of what we're doing and why we're stuck out here in this wilderness."

"Ah," John sighed. "Yes, I think I understand. Look, besides this special wrestling of mine that impressed the captain so much, I have some ideas for weapons that I think you could use. You've seen these new-fangled guns, haven't you?"

"Yes. We even have a few."

"Well, I've been working on an improvement. How would you like to have a gun that could shoot a hundred bullets at a time, as quickly as you wanted, and without having to reload?"

"Can you make something like that?"

"No, but I can tell your smiths how to make it. It's basically a matter of feeding the bullets in from a hopper. We'd use revolving barrels so that the heat won't burn them out. We could call this a machine gun."

"It sounds . . . you know, it sounds as though it might actually work." The general's eyes lit up like a small boy's at Christmas. "Captain," he said, "how about arranging suitable quarters for Lieutenant Harlen and his aide? And see if you can hustle up something for them to eat. They must be hungry after their journey. Now, John, tell me more about this machine gun of yours."

They talked about weapons and strategy for more than four hours.

12

John soon fell in with the routine of camp life. The day started at six-thirty with a bugle call, which was followed in half an hour by a bowl of gruel-like mess that passed for breakfast. After breakfast came the normal housekeeping chores from which John and Hurd were exempted. The men spent the day drilling. John spent the morning with the camp metalsmiths building a working model of the machine gun, and the afternoon giving lessons in judo to a special class. Every so often a raiding party would go out to pick up needed supplies.

Thus three months passed. John and Hurd were too closely watched to try to escape, and after a while John began to think it might be more profitable for them to stay with the Army anyhow.

When the machine gun was finished John demonstrated it to the general. He was very impressed. "How many of these can you make?" he asked.

"About one every three weeks."

"Fine. Excellent. Lieutenant Harlen, would you be good enough to dine with me tonight?"

"I would consider it a privilege."

At dinner that night the general and John discussed the future plans for the People's Army. ". . . and in about three years I should be ready to come out in the open," the general was saying.

"But sir, why do you plan to wait three years? It seems to me—"

"I have," the general interrupted, "at the present time approximately eight hundred men. I can't possibly face an army in the field with eight hundred men, no matter how well-trained they are."

"It isn't really necessary to face an opposing army in the field," John said slowly. "I have heard of a form of fighting that it seems your men are in a very good position to use." The general leaned forward. This man seemed to be full of ideas.

Slowly, and in great detail, John explained the concept of guerrilla warfare to the general. Hit and run fighting. Hitting small posts with a superior force and disappearing before reinforcements could arrive. Conducting a propaganda campaign among the peasants. Making every farm a base of supply and every farmer an agent. Instead of meeting the enemy in force, harassing him at every turn. Striking at one place tonight and at another place a hundred sterbs away tomorrow.

General Garth sat and listened like a man in a trance. When John finished, the general started throwing questions at him, question following question like bullets from the new machine gun. And, "How long will it take you to train a unit in these guerrilla tactics?" was his final question.

Three months later, John and Hurd led a dozen men into the first authentic guerrilla raid in the history of Lyff. Their target was a small Guard station just outside the village of Penchdarg.

"Remember," he cautioned his men, "the important things are speed and shock. Don't give 'em time to figure out what's happening. Hit and run and hit again. They outnumber us two to one, and if you give 'em time to think, we've had it."

Actually, the situation wasn't all that serious. To begin with, the guerrillas were armed with dynamite grenades and four machine guns. The garrison could have been manned by a whole Embrace and still the guerrillas would have had the greater fire-power. But this was as much a training exercise as it was a raid, and John wanted to keep his men on their toes.

Under cover of darkness, the fourteen rebels crept up to within a few yards of the garrison. The sentry route was less than an arm's length away. Soon a solitary guardsman, annoyed at having sentry duty but not expecting any trouble, strolled past in a thoroughly unmilitary fashion. A shadow rose behind him, struck silently, and the sentry fell to the ground.

John made a clucking sound with his tongue, and six guerrillas moved like a ragged black wave toward the garrison and vanished. Fifteen seconds later, John clucked again, and the second wave moved in, leaving John and Hurd alone in the scrubby woods.

John counted slowly to himself in a low, hissing whisper, and Hurd tensely held his breath. Except for the whispering, the night was coldly still. The few nocturnal creatures Lyff had developed were, without exception, silent, and the silence was as tangible as cloth. John Harlen whispered, "Seventy-five," and then screamed as though the history of agony were in him.

At once the night fell apart in explosions, short and skillful chatters of machine-gun fire, frequent single shots and a continuing, unbroken maniacal yell.

The guardsmen were too sleepily terrified to offer any worthwhile resistance. In spite of the noise and the destruction, the principal job the guerrillas found themselves saddled with was rounding up and guarding frightened prisoners.

While as many guerrillas as could be spared from guard duty busied themselves with the orderly looting of the garrison, John Harlen addressed the twenty-eight half-dressed Mother's Guards. "Lyffans," he proclaimed, "you have been defeated and your lives have been spared by the People's Army. You can not stand against us because Mother stands with us. Her cause and ours are the same: Lyff belongs to all of Mother's children. Mother cries out, 'Set my children free,' and we are Mother's helpers, to do her word."

He turned away from them and strode toward the nearest building. As he reached the door, he turned once more and shouted, "Lyff for all Lyffans!" As the guerrillas echoed his shout, he disappeared into the building.

Hurd was trying bravely not to laugh as John entered the room. "Mother's nose, John Harlen," he said. "Talk about hams—"

"Do you think I overdid it?"

"No, I just think you enjoyed it too much."

John grinned. "Back home I used to be a poet."

"That's logical," Hurd said. "Are we ready to go home now?"

"We should be." John gave another prodigious yell, which was answered by a chorus of yelps. "Yep, we're ready."

"Yes, you're enjoying this altogether too much."

They gathered in the courtyard, where the shocked guardsmen were bound each to a separate tree or pillar. One of the guerrillas handed John a dripping brush, and John painted a stick drawing of an upraised sword on the nearest wall. Then they mounted their loot-laden dalbers, shouted once more, "Lyff for all Lyffans," and skittered off into the darkness.

The stunning success of the guerrilla raids proved to the Lyffan authorities as nothing else could have that the People's Army was not just another gang of mountain bandits. The Anti-Conspiracy Committee immediately identified the rebels as paid agents of the Conspiracy, and soon the Committee put a small army in the field to combat the guerrilla menace. This army was commanded by Tchornyo Gar-Spolnyen Hiirlte, who was scared witless.

Other measures were also taken. After vainly trying to increase enlistments, the King's Army instituted a draft, and official estimates were that a fighting army might well be ready for action in little more than a year. Unofficial but more accurate estimates were less optimistic.

The Telegraph Trust rushed squads of specially trained

company police to every telegraph office within the guerrillas' operating range.

Meanwhile, it became a capital crime to write, print, paint or cause otherwise to be displayed on any wall, either public or private, the words "Lyff for all Lyffans," or the image of a sword.

The Committee sent investigating groups to every city and town in Lyff to ferret out conspirators. These groups operated on the belief that accusation was proof of the crime, and thousands of conspirators were jailed and, eventually, tried. Fear of the investigators entered everybody's life. A chance word misinterpreted might lead to arrest and ruin, and no one dared to speak. Worse, no one dared to be silent, for silence might become suspicious, and so each man's least word was a deep risk.

Soon the People's Army had more recruits than it could handle. There was actually a waiting list. The training program ran in shifts from dawn to dawn, and the smiths were only able to meet the demand for weapons because so many smiths enlisted.

The raids gradually became battles, the battles very slowly became campaigns. The first guerrilla bands were seldom larger than fourteen men, but three and a half years later movements involving a thousand men were commonplace.

"There's nothing stimulates a culture more than a good, brisk war now and then," John explained to Hurd one day. "Each side has to be constantly inventing weapons faster than the other side can invent defenses and inventing defenses against the other side's new weapons. A lot of useful discoveries get made under a forced draft like that."

Harlen, naturally, spent most of his time inventing weapons. He was in competition not only with the guilds of Lyff, but also with the rest of his own Special Detail. But the inventive process soon got out of control, and though John did manage to avoid inventing nuclear explosives, he was not able to avoid inventing the burner, a vicious little hand weapon based on the laser principle.

Finally, after three and a half years of hit-and-run fighting, General Garth decided that it was time for the People's Army to take and hold some towns. The first town to be taken, he decided, would be a near-by trading center called Astindarg.

13

The People's Army marched in force toward Astindarg. Two regiments of infantry, with assorted cavalry and artillery units mixed among them, made a moving column of men four sterbs long on the main road. The town garrison only held two Embraces of Mother's Guards, but General Garth wanted to make an impressive showing of force. The general and John were riding in the first column, receiving information from the screen of scouts out in front, and passing instructions back to the troops behind them.

When they were about a half-hour's march outside the city, one of the scouts came riding up to the column at a dead heat.

"I've just come from a hill overlooking Astindarg," he said, throwing the general a hasty salute, "and the whole Mother-lorn town's on fire."

The general gave a rapid series of orders for the army to halt in its tracks and wait for further instructions, and then he and John followed the scout back to the observation point.

"Right over this hill, sir, you can see the whole thing." The scout led them to the crest of a hill and pointed at the town on the other side. "You see what I mean sir? The whole town's burning." The general and John peered over the edge of the hill.

John was the first to notice a peculiar fact about the burning town. "Look sir," he said to the general, "the whole town isn't burning yet. It looks like the fire was set in a straight line through the center of town from right to left." John pointed, his hand moving in an arc to illustrate what he meant. When it reached the end of the arc his hand suddenly froze, pointing outside of town on the left, and he said several loud words in a language the general didn't understand.

"What is it?" the general asked. He looked where John was pointing. There was a large, shining, metallic-looking object sitting on the grass beyond the town. "And what in Mother's Name is *that*?"

"A spaceship," John answered, "and a good five years early."

"A what?"

"Listen, call for all artillery units that have heavy-duty heat beams and for as much of the cavalry as we can get here in a hurry. I'll explain while they're coming. It looks like we've got a real fight on our hands!"

The spaceship's pilot made his way to the main cabin of the ship where his passengers were assembled. "We've landed, gentlemen," he announced.

"So I notice," one of the four passengers said. "We also seem to have set a town on fire doing it."

The pilot gave him a hard stare. "I'm used to concrete landing fields," he said. "If you had told me where we were heading at the beginning instead of keeping it a secret and making me change course at the last minute, I would have told you to get another pilot. One who was accustomed to landing on grass fields. Maybe a Navy boy, they do it all the time."

The passenger snorted. "I've already explained to you that we're a special investigating committee acting under authority of Senator Walsh. We're investigating a contact violation by the Navy. Do you really think we could come here in a Navy ship?"

"It seems to me," said the pilot, "that we're doing a bit of contact violation ourselves just by being here."

"But I've already told you we're a special investigating

committee," the passenger said impatiently. "It's a different situation."

"Oh, I see. You Consies made the rule, so of course it's perfectly okay for you to break it. Logic. Simple. Why didn't *I* think of that?" The pilot made a face as though he were tasting something unpleasant, but before any of the others could reply, he said, "Well, I guess you heroes ought to step outside now and see if the natives are friendly. Although, I admit they might be just a bit perturbed about the burning of their town." He made an about face and retreated into the pilot's cabin.

The four professional busybodies went outside. The townspeople seemed to be ignoring them. "They don't seem to be very curious, Stepan," one of them said. "It's almost as if they're used to seeing spaceships land in their backyard."

Stepan, the leader of the group, turned to his comrade. "It could be," he said, "it just could be, Alain, that they're too busy fighting the fire to come out and socialize." Alain looked properly chastised.

Stepan looked around at the quiet countryside surrounding the town. "I wonder," he said, "how hard it is going to be to prove illegal contact. They can't have done much in five years."

There was a peculiar coughing sound from behind a nearby hill. Suddenly a loud whine filled the air. Alain looked at Stepan in alarm. "It sounds like a generator," he said.

"It does at that, sort of," Stepan replied cautiously.

A laser beam shot out from behind the hill and cut off the nose of their ship.

"What the . . . ." Stepan gasped.

A large body of men riding what looked like midget dinosaurs came charging over the hill with spears at ready. The men were yelling, and the dinosaurs were gronching, and the Terrans were frozen in place more from shock, as one of them explained later, than from fear. It was a bloodless victory.

14

The day after the Gar-Terrayens' anniversary party, the Fifth and Seventh Regiments of the King's Army marched off toward Astindarg. The troops, armed with the very latest weapons and thoroughly trained in their use, were among the most deadly fighters Lyff had ever produced. Other units, notified by telegraph, joined them along the way, and by the time the king's forces reached the hills outside Astindarg three days later, they formed a marching column six men wide by five and a half sterbs long.

At the end of the third day they made camp in rough battle formation on the slopes leading to the town. The spaceship was clearly visible, even though it was several sterbs away and smoke from the still-burning town filled the air. None of the king's men slept easily that night.

The battle began before dawn the next morning with a heavy artillery barrage. The forces holding Astindarg responded with war rockets and heat beams. The air was crushed under the constant roar of exploding shells, the shrill racket of passing rockets, and the soft but heavy crackling hiss of the laser beams.

"I'll tell you what," men in the ranks whispered to each other. "I don't like this one Mother-lorn bit. Them dalberson spacemen 'as got shells what shoots themselves. It just ain't natural."

The order to advance was given an hour after dawn, and the king's men, nervous, moved slowly, even stealthily, through the smoke-stained, bomb-brightened morning. They were armed as variously as warriors in a circus pageant. Some carried high-powered rifles, some bazookas, but more carried older weapons. Crossbows, lances, broadswords and axes were more common than firearms, and some men even carried useless shields gaily decorated with their family crests.

The advance on Astindarg moved too slowly, and neither bugle calls nor their officers' exhortations could make the men move faster. The machine guns on the town walls were cutting down the king's men faster than they could be replaced. Finally the newly commissioned general, Ansgar Sorenstein, mounted his dalber and dashed into the field ahead of the troops.

"Follow me," he shouted, and the king's men rallied around him and followed him up to the walls of Astindarg. Suddenly, just as Ansgar and his soldiers reached the gates, a silence fell upon the battleground that was heavier than the racket it replaced.

"They've ceased firing, sir," Ansgar's orderly said with the ghost of a salute.

"Yes, and so have we. Now what in Mother's Name is going on?"

In spite of the danger, John Harlen, Hurd and General Garth watched the battle from the roof of the Temple, the highest vantage point Astindarg could provide.

"Impressive," John muttered.

"Do you think we can hold them off?" asked the general.

"We should be able to. If the rockets don't decide it for us, the laser beams will. What bothers me is that there are so many people out there. So many of them are going to be killed."

"That's what war is all about," the general answered sadly. "You might as well get used to it now."

"Hey, John," Hurd broke in. "Who is that out front? I mean the officer on the dalber?"

"I don't know, Hurd. He looks familiar, though. Here, let me see that telescope."

John took a long look through the glass, then whistled

softly. "Hurd," he said, "pass the word to cease fire. Run up the white flag. That's Ansgar Sorenstein out there."

"The thing is," Ansgar said, "we thought we were fighting aliens. If I'd only stopped to think, I'd have realized that it was a Federation ship, but the possibility never entered my mind."

They were meeting in a hastily jury-rigged telegraph office in the Temple. While they talked, a technician soldered connections, tested circuits, and as quickly as possible restored the telegraph to working order.

"That's what we thought, too," John admitted. "In fact, we didn't realize it was a Federation ship until after we'd disabled it."

"A Conservationist investigating committee." Ansgar sighed. "If it wasn't so Mother-lorn silly, it'd almost be tragic."

"The line is clear now, sirs," the technician announced respectfully.

"Great. How good are you at sending code, Ansgar? I'm afraid I've grown rusty these last four years."

"Good enough, I suppose. What do you want to send?"

Together they composed a report of the battle and what preceded it. John added a few terse paragraphs describing his activities with the People's Army. Although they tried to keep their report as short as possible, it took forty-five minutes to transmit.

Outside, the men of the King's Army mingled cautiously with the men of the People's Army. No one knew what was happening, of course, and everyone found it hard to get used to being friendly toward yesterday's enemies. Consequently, the mingling exhibited all the rigid formality of an ancient dance.

Thanks to Pindar Smith, none of the soldiers had any trouble getting used to the idea of spaceships. Smith had invented science fiction three years before, establishing, in fact, a Lyffan edition of *Advanced Science Fiction and Theories,* and every literate Lyffan was a fan.

The most confused member of the People's Army, however, was General Garth. He knew Motherless well that the king's men were by nature his enemies. He had lived with that idea for more than twenty years. To be told in the midst of a battle that the king's men were really on his side was too much for him. He wandered through the town wearing a dazed look and refusing to answer questions. He couldn't tell whether his life was falling apart around him or reaching its glorious climax, but whichever was happening, he knew he didn't like it.

Ansgar signaled the end of his transmission and leaned back tiredly. But before he touched the back of the chair, the telegraph was calling for attention.

As John took down the message, his expression grew grimmer and grimmer. "Civil war," it said. "Anti-Conspiracy forces attacking palace. Lyffdarg in turmoil. Send help soonest."

Without a word, John dashed out to find General Garth.

The next day at dawn the newly organized King's and People's Army fell into marching formation in the Astindarg town square. "Lyffans," shouted John in his best demagogic tones, "there is civil war in Lyffdarg. Traitorous nobles seeking to overthrow the king are even now laying waste to the city. Thousands of innocent civilians have been slaughtered, Mother's Temple has been defiled, and Mother's Law has been defied. Let the differences between us be forgotten in our opposition to our common enemy. Lyff for all Lyffans! Long live the King!"

The mightiest army ever assembled on Lyff marched forth with songs and patriotic slogans.

15

Tchornyo finally met his mysterious benefactor late on the night of the Gar-Terrayens' party. He was unceremoniously awakened and escorted to Committee headquarters by the dark little man who'd acted so long as go-between for the Committee and the anonymous nobleman.

"What's this all about?" he asked the little man several times as they rode through the darkened streets of Lyffdarg, but the little man refused to answer.

When the mysterious noble entered his office, Tchornyo fell to his knees almost by reflex.

"Sit down, Tchornyo," the noble said kindly. "We have much to talk about and no time for formalities."

Tchornyo sat down meekly and listened while the noble, pacing slowly back and forth in the narrow room, described his plans for the Committee.

"Tomorrow morning," he said, "the Fifth and Seventh Regiments will depart for Astindarg. That will leave three Embraces of Guards and one regiment of the King's Army to guard Lyffdarg. We can't expect to find the city so loosely held again."

"Yes sir," Tchornyo said inanely.

"Now here is what you have to do. The regiments are scheduled to leave at dawn. Two hours later, you are to attack the Guards barracks in force. You shouldn't need more than a thousand men."

"But sir, Mother's Guards—"

"Mother's Guards are only soldiers. While you're attacking the barracks, have your friend Gardnyen take another two thousand men and attack the palace. Both attacks must be successful."

"The palace?"

"That's right. And when you're finished with the barracks, bring your men to the palace and assist Gardnyen."

"But sir, the king!" Tchornyo was in an agony of confusion.

"Mother blast the king," the noble said coldly. "Tomorrow we shall overthrow the king."

"But the king is my uncle!" Tchornyo wanted to cry.

"Rubbish. The king is your enemy. Who do you think is behind this conspiracy you've been fighting for the past four and a half years?"

"The king?"

"Of course the king. Who else would benefit from a conspiracy against the nobility? Osgard has been trying to reduce our strength ever since his father's death. *You* know that. I don't care if he's your own brother—"

"My mother's brother, sir."

"Mother's kneecap, Tchornyo, I know that. All I'm trying to say is that if you want to combat the conspiracy, you have to fight King Osgard. He's the conspirator. It's as simple as that."

"But I can't fight my own uncle, sir. And besides, he's the king. Do you want me to commit treason?"

"It's only treason if you lose, Tchornyo. And do you realize what I can do to you if you don't fight? If I wanted to, I could denounce you as a traitor. The king still trusts me, and everyone would believe me. Furthermore, I can prove it from your Committee's membership records. You've been very careless about screening recruits.

"But that's not what I'll do if you disobey me. I have more intimate ways to punish such insubordination. The Long Death can last six months as easily as it lasts one."

There was a period of silence during which the nobleman stood at the window and stared out over the city while Tchornyo sat like a statue at his desk, trying to reach a decision. The nobleman turned around suddenly and snapped, "Well?"

"I'll give the orders now," Tchornyo muttered weakly.

"Splendid," the nobleman beamed. "I knew I could count on you. Now I have to hurry back home. I'll see you tomorrow afternoon at the palace. Kneel down so that I can bless you."

Suppressing a feeling of acute vertigo, Tchornyo knelt beside his desk. The High Priest and Father of the Fathers invoked Mother's blessing on the coming insurrection and then departed hastily.

"Did it work?" someone asked the High Priest.

"Like a charm," he answered. "I simply appealed to the boy's higher nature and he agreed to everything."

"Meaning that you threatened him with torture, I suppose."

"Something like that."

"If I didn't know you better, I'd accuse you of crudity."

"My methods may seem a bit crude at times, but my results are always subtle."

"Indeed. And what do you plan to do about the boy afterward?"

"Nothing, of course. If we succeed, nothing need be done, and if we fail, nothing can be done. In either event, young Tchornyo will not be a problem."

Two hours after dawn, a thousand Committeemen stormed the barracks while two thousand more besieged the palace. Half an hour later, five thousand enraged Lyffdargers attacked the Committeemen.

That afternoon Tchornyo issued a call for reinforcements. Committee detachments from all the neighboring towns and villages hurried to their leader's aid.

The battle at the city gates lasted three days and nights. Finally the poorly armed commoners were forced to give way, and the Committeemen streamed through the city like a tide of fire.

Because the Committeemen had no training in house-to-house combat, the battle raged for three more days. Snipers picked off the brilliantly uniformed Committeemen with insulting ease, but the Committeemen had little luck in picking off the snipers. Hundreds of noble families were left without heirs and the power of the nobility was in danger of being destroyed forever. With this in mind, Tchornyo finally gave orders to burn down the city.

The first building was fired early in the morning of the seventh day of the insurrection. The smoke rose into the clear sky like a dark and greasy battle flag. The Lyffdargers defended their homes fiercely, and each fire cost from five to a dozen noble lives. By midday, only fifteen buildings were in flames, one city block.

Just before midday, watchers on the city walls saw a cloud on the horizon. As the hours passed and the flames spread, the cloud grew larger, until even the weakest eyes could identify it as the dust raised by an approaching army.

Tchornyo's hopes grew as the army drew near. These troops must surely be the reinforcements he'd been praying for the whole week long. Near dusk his hopes fell again with a final, crashing fall. The King's and People's Army charged the gates and crashed through, swords gleaming, rifles blazing and laser beams hissing hungrily, swarming into the city like a horde of angry angels of destruction. And worst of all, the killers from the five-years-distant alley rode at the head of that fearsome company.

The insurrection promptly dissolved in a rabbit chase. All through the city, gibbering Committeemen fled in terror, seeking cover not only in buildings they were prepared to burn a few hours earlier, but also in buildings that were already aflame. Dozens of Committeemen died in fires they themselves had set.

The Committeemen fled, and following came, fierce as righteousness, the king's men, the guerrillas, and the maddened populace. The people ran thick with fury, and the gutters ran thick with blood.

By nightfall it was over.

John Harlen found Tchornyo sitting alone in the darkness of his office at Committee headquarters.

"Whoever you are, come on in," Tchornyo said wearily when he heard John moving around in the outer office.

John went in and turned on the lights.

"So it's you," Tchornyo said. "I thought it would be. My luck seems to run that way. I suppose you've come to kill me." His voice expressed nothing but inhuman exhaustion.

"Kill you?" John said heartily. "Nonsense. I'm here to convert you. If nothing else, this adventure has probably made a man of you, and we need men."

Their conversation lasted several hours.

16

Lyffdarg did not return to normal after the fighting stopped. The defeat of the Anti-Conspiracy Committee, which broke the nobility's hold on the commoners, precipitated a political crisis that kept the city in a state of turmoil for six months. With the nobles so weakened, it was necessary to form a new government, and the commoners insisted on their new-found right to participate in the enterprise.

From dawn to dusk, impassioned orators made every corner clangorous with argument. "The best government is the least government," some of them proclaimed. "And the least government is none at all. Hurrah for anarchy and the new millennium!"

"Dalber chips," other speakers retorted. "These dalberson anarchists think that without government every man will be a king, but you and I know better. Anarchy means that no man will be king, not even in his own home. It may be true that the best government is the least government, but it is most certainly true that the worst government is no government at all."

But the political ferment attending the birth of a constitutional monarchy was neither the only source of excitement in Lyffdarg nor the greatest. This honor was reserved for Special Detail L-2.

The fact that a spaceship had landed near Astindarg could not be kept secret. Too many men had seen the ship and spoken to its passengers. Therefore, John Harlen reasoned, it was no longer necessary or useful to keep the Special Detail secret. The whole story of the Special

Detail's mission was printed once a week for two months in Ansgar Sorenstein's Lyffdarg *Chronicle,* along with an appeal to all Lyffans to help the Terrans prepare for the coming invasion.

The popularity of Pindar Smith's science-fiction magazine paid off. For three years Lyffans had been reading about adventures in space, and they greeted this sudden change from fantasy to fact with overwhelming enthusiasm. The Guild of Guilds sent a delegation of master craftsmen to Astindarg to study the Federation spaceship. A series of lectures on the history of the Federation offered by the Special Detail was so heavily oversubscribed that it had to be repeated twice. Hurd Gar-Olnyn Saarlip wrote and Pindar Smith published a fanciful long poem on the beauties of space travel, and it sold out the day it was issued.

The greatest demonstration of Lyffan enthusiasm took place in the most unexpected manner possible six months after the fall of the Committee. In the first free elections ever held on Lyff, the people gave Hurd the office of prime minister, even though he hadn't campaigned for the post.

"My friends," he said in his inaugural address, "we have come through a time of great crisis, only to face a greater crisis yet. Even now nameless invaders, bent only on destruction, are hurtling through interstellar space toward our fair planet. Our course is clear, and I pledge myself and the government you have chosen me to lead to the pursuit of this course. First we must arm ourselves to drive off this new enemy. This will be done. Second, we must prepare ourselves to take our rightful place in the Terran Federation. This will be done.

"I say to you now that the past is no more than a graveyard. The glory of Lyff lies in the future. The glory of Lyff will be found between the stars. In Mother's Secret Name, I promise that we shall all share in the coming glory. Lyff for all Lyffans! The future is ours!" The applause lasted almost an hour.

"Mother's nose, Hurd," John said later. "Talk about hams—"

"Do you think I overdid it?"

"No, I just think you enjoyed it too much."

Hurd grinned. "Yeah," he said, "it was kind of fun."

17

"Senator Walsh would like to see you, sir."

"Oh, Good Lord," Admiral Bellman muttered, "again? Why does he have to arrive so precisely at tea time? Show the senator in, Harry. And bring in another cup and saucer, too."

"Yes sir." The yeoman ducked out of the office and returned almost immediately with a tea cup, Senator Walsh, and a saucer. That the cup and saucer didn't match was an act of criticism on the yeoman's part.

"Edvalt," the senator said in lieu of greetings, "when was the last time you heard from your precious Special Detail?"

"There is no Special Detail."

"I know, I know. When did it report last?"

"It hasn't reported yet. Secrecy, you know. I expect to be receiving a report sometime this year."

"You're in trouble."

"I'm always in trouble. That's what I get paid for. What is it this time?"

"A little less than a year ago the Conservationist Party sent an expedition to Lyff."

"You did *what*?"

"I said, we sent an expedition to Lyff and— Now see what you've done. You've spilt your tea. Why are you always so nervous, Edvalt?"

"Damn the tea! How did you people find out about Lyff?"

"We have ways."

"Don't you just. Tell me about this expedition."

"Just one ship, Ed, five men. The important thing is this: they reported that they were about to land, and they haven't reported since."

After a reflective pause, Admiral Bellman said, "So?"

"Those people are in trouble on Lyff. They may even be dead."

Bellman repeated his previous question.

Senator Walsh's temper began to slip. "All I want to know is, what are you going to do about it?"

"What am I going to do? Why, nothing, of course. Why should I do anything?"

"Those five men are Federation citizens, Bellman. If they're in trouble, it's your duty to help them."

"No, you're wrong there, Emsley. Those five men are criminals. I don't have any duties toward them at all. Why don't you report this to the police?"

"What do you mean, criminals?"

"Careful there. A man your age can't afford to fly into rages like that."

"I'm only ninety-one, damn it. I've got at least thirty good years left. Now just what do you mean by calling my men criminals?"

"You say they landed on Lyff. Since Lyff is still quarantined, that means they're guilty of a contact violation. If they're in trouble, that's their problem. The Navy can't be expected to go barreling around the galaxy in aid of a pack of common criminals. No, not at a time like this. Tell it to the police."

"But . . . but. . . ." The old man was speechless with rage. He dashed around the office like a one-legged polka dancer, fighting to regain his self-control. Finally he stood still, clenched his fists, shook himself, and shouted, "Now you've done it! Contact violation! You won't get away with this, Bellman, I'm warning you." With that he dashed out of the office and was gone.

"Amazingly agile for such an old man," Bellman chuckled. He felt better than he'd felt in years.

Still chuckling, he wiped spilled tea off the document

he'd been reading when the senator arrived. The document, actually a sixty-four page booklet, bore the title: *Special Detail L-2—First Interim Report*. Bellman leafed through it until he reached that passage describing the capture of the Consie investigators, and then he laughed until his worried yeoman came in to ask if anything was wrong.

18

With the threat of imminent invasion and awareness of the Terran Federation for stimuli, Lyffan technological development surged forward like a dalber sensing food, and everyone was amazed but the Lyffans. Almost overnight the Guild of Guilds became a giant industrial combine, and individual workshops became pilot plants or research laboratories.

The Lyffans took the Consie spaceship apart piece by piece, and then put it back together again. They set themselves the task of duplicating or improving upon everything the ship contained. What proved difficult to copy, they duplicated in six months; what proved impossible to duplicate, they replaced with their own inventions. Then they set out to build a truly Lyffan spaceship.

New guilds sprang up like flowers. The first of these, the Guild of Engineers, was followed in short order by the Guild of Electronicians, the Guild of Mathematicians, the Guild of Optical Engineers, and, oddly enough, the Guild of Scripturalists. These were not so much guilds as they were scientific academies. There was even a Guild of Physicists.

Soon Lyffan scientists were mapping the face of Poor Sister, one of the nearer planets, with a laser-beam radar. Another group of scientists developed a digital computer. The first model weighed almost a ton, but the second model weighed only three pounds.

All Lyff was gripped by a creative obsession that was stronger than mere insanity. No one was immune. The unskilled man in the street was as likely to produce a basic invention as the most skilled member of the Guild of Guilds. The secrets of the universe were suddenly, it seemed, made available for the asking, and there was no man on Lyff who did not ask.

Prime Minister Hurd Gar-Olnyn Saarlip made frequent, passionate speeches urging the people on to new and, necessarily, better achievements, but these speeches were cheerfully dismissed—or accepted, if you prefer—as the political propaganda they so obviously were. The Lyffans were achieving more and faster than anyone could keep track of already.

"What I don't understand," John told Hurd one day, "is how your people have managed to adjust to this situation so easily. Six years ago Lyff was a simple agricultural planet without even a worthwhile hint of modern technology, and now look. You've become a race of engineers. But how did you do it?"

"I thought I explained all this six years ago."

"If you did, I must have missed it. How about explaining it again for me."

"All right. In *The Book of Garth Gar-Muyen Garth,* whom Mother—"

"Hold on, old son. Theology?"

"Not really. Anyhow, there are many sections of the Book that were obscure before you Terrans came here. One section in particular was so obscure that we thought it was dealing with ethics until you people told us about electricity. Then everything suddenly made sense. The name of that section is, 'A Handbook of Modern Physics,' and the best minds on Lyff were unable to make any sense from it before."

There was a long silence. This was not the sort of explanation John had been expecting, and he wasn't sure, now that he had it, that he really wanted it. Finally, however, his scientific curiosity defeated his native caution, and he said, "Hurd, where can I get hold of a copy of *The Book of Garth Gar-Muyen Garth?*"

"Whom Mother loves. Why don't you ask the High Priest?"

General Garth was made commander of the still non-existent space fleet, and started training crews to man ships and use weapons that had yet to be invented. "If we wait for the Mother-lorn engineers to invent the ships," he explained, "we won't have time to train the men. This way maybe we can finish the ships and the crews at the same time."

Weapons research was an especially fertile enterprise. Within a year the weapons developed by John Harlen for the People's Army and by the Guild of Guilds and the rest of the Special Detail for the King's Army were obsolete. The men who mapped Poor Sister's face with a laser beam radar later used the same laser beams to blast Poor Sister's face to molten ruin.

Pressor and tractor beams, old and futile dreams of Federation scientists, were developed to facilitate the handling of heavy metal spaceship parts. Their utility as weapons was discovered by accident.

Acting on poorly understood hints in *The Book of Garth Gar-Muyen Garth*, the Guild of Electronicians developed a series of so-called "phase guns." These were all failures from the technical point of view; the inventors were hoping to convert matter into energy, but instead the phase guns converted energy into matter. Disappointed but undaunted, the Electronicians renamed their phase guns "entropy devices" and attacked the problem from another angle. It took one more year for somebody to notice that the entropy devices could be adjusted to convert any kind of energy into almost any kind of matter.

Because they were mainly concerned with the development of Lyffan space vehicles, the Terrans paid relatively little attention to the new weapons. The basic assumption was that the Lyffan ships would be armed with Federation weapons.

"As a matter of fact, the prime minister was quite right," the High Priest and Father of the Fathers said. "Indeed, it's possible that the scientific content of *The Book of Garth Gar-Muyen Garth* is responsible for the current religious revival. Even though it is no longer mandatory, attendance at Temple services has increased markedly since the fall of the Committee."

All this talk about religion embarrassed John. He was a Rational Materialist, of course, and held the superstitious belief that religion is nothing but superstition. "I'm glad your attendance has increased," he said, almost as though he cared, "but what interests me most at the moment is *The Book of Garth*. Do you know where I can get hold of a copy?"

"You don't know much about our religion, do you?"

"Well . . . No, not really. You see, I've had so many other things to do—"

"What a pity. I'm sure you'd find it to be a most sympathetic faith. Here, let me give you a copy of *The Book of Garth*. Maybe it will stimulate your interest."

19

The scout ship was in trouble. Even to someone completely ignorant of space craft it would have been obvious that the scout ship was not acting normally. It alternated aimless bursts of acceleration with hours of total immobility. Sometimes it seemed to waver, as though it were about to dissolve. To anyone who knew about such things, it would have been equally obvious, even without knowing what propulsion system was involved, that the ship was suffering from a severely polarized drive.

The ship was on picket duty with the advanced fleet of the Migration. It was not operated by what we would call people, for the Migrants were so nonhumanoid that, though thoroughly material, they could only be described in mathematical equations. They were exactly what they called themselves: Migrants. They were hunting for a home.

They were also an implacable army, or, if you wish, a plague, for anything that was not the home they hunted and anything that interfered with their search, in short, anything they came upon that was not themselves, they destroyed. And not in anger or because of some inate hostility, but simply as a matter of routine. What they could not use, they destroyed. It had always been thus.

The Migrant scout was in trouble and needed a landing place.

It was like dawn at midnight. The people of Prymilbos were awakened by a sound they did not hear, a tearing of the fabric of the atmosphere so loud it was inaudible. This was followed by a faint glow in the sky that grew rapidly brighter and brighter until it was painful to look at. That was the last thing the eight thousand people of Prymilbos ever saw.

In Lyffdarg, the noise was audible. It sounded like the first crack of a nearby lightning bolt sustained for an impossibly long time. And instead of a dawnlike glow in the sky, the Lyffdargers saw a definite and clearly defined light, like a vagrant sun, rushing through the sky toward the distant seacoast.

"That's one hell of a meteor," Ansgar Sorenstein said.

"I hope that's what it is," John answered glumly.

Then the whole sky brightened and a fan of intense light spread from horizon to horizon.

John started counting under his breath, as he had when timing guerrilla attacks. When the shock wave and the sound had passed, shaking Lyffdarg like a handkerchief, John said, "Nine hundred sterbs. That would be Prymilbos. See if you can raise Prymilbos on the radio."

But all the radio could pick up was a hissing static that sounded like surf after a storm.

The Royal Lyffan Army, successor to the People's Army and the King's Army, sent a force to Prymilbos that left Lyffdarg three hours before dawn. Instead of marching, the RLA rode steam-powered trucks and tanks, and was able to reach the seacoast town just a few hours after midday.

Only, Prymilbos wasn't there anymore. Where it had stood there was now an enormous, steaming crater.

"Well," John said, "that settles the meteor idea. Look."

Beyond the crater, mostly hidden by the steam and smoke, a long, thin spaceship stood on its tail like a gleaming tower.

"And unless something very strange has happened since we left Terra," Ansgar remarked, "that's not one of our ships at all."

There was a sudden sharp crackling noise, and the front of the advancing RLA column disappeared. The rest of the unit stopped and dispersed into the underbrush. Heat-beam technicians labored to drag their heavy weapons off the road. The sharp crackling noise happened again, and a dozen empty trucks vanished.

Then everything was quiet. The heat-beam technicians worked silently, not even taking time out to swear. With infinite care they assembled their gigantic lasers, moving slowly and making sure that each step was done correctly. They might have been in a laboratory instead of a battle, they worked so carefully.

Finally one of the beams was ready. The technicians, still moving with painful precision, aimed it at the distant ship and fired a long blast.

The nose of the Migrant scout turned cherry red, then white, and then vaporized.

The poisonous air of Lyff rushed through the ship like a tide of death. Everything the noxious oxygen touched rusted or, if living, died. The Migrants themselves burst into brilliant yellow flames in the corrosive atmosphere, and there were no survivors.

When the Lyffans reached the ship, most of the more violent chemical activity had stopped. John tested the area for radioactivity, found nothing bothersome, and led a squad aboard the enemy scout.

There was no sign of the Migrants themselves. They had been throughly consumed in their own flames. Almost all of the ship's equipment had been ruined by exposure to the atmosphere, but the Lyffan technicians felt sure they could reconstruct in their own way almost all of the oxidized instruments and weapons.

John thought so, too. His first act when he returned to Lyffdarg was to break a regulation he'd observed with religious strictness for more than seven years. He sent an emergency message to Terra.

ENEMY SHIP CAPTURED ON LYFF.

Admiral Bellman was in trouble. The message allowed him no doubt about what he had to do, but how to do it was a problem. He couldn't send one ship to Lyff, let alone the armada of fighters and scientists the occasion demanded, without letting the Consies learn about Special Detail L-2, which would result in his almost instant court martial.

Just as he was about to decide to make that sacrifice, an inspiration struck him. He dialed a number on the visiphone. When the screen cleared, he said, "Good morning, Senator Walsh. Remember those friends of yours who got in trouble on Lyff? Well, I've just figured out a way to rescue them."

20

The Migrant ship was that last little impetus the Lyffan scientists needed. The wealth of new ideas the ship provided, plus the fact that it had wantonly destroyed a Lyffan city, resulted in less than a month in not a spaceship, but a space fleet.

The Terrans didn't realize how advanced Lyff had become until the Guild of Guilds invited them to witness a space-drive test, and even then all they realized was that they hadn't realized how advanced Lyff had become. The test itself completed their education.

"Our problem is mainly one of choice," they were told before the test by Gelph Gar-Pandyen Teeltl, chancellor of the Guild of Physicists. "We have a number of devices that can power a ship available to us, but we won't know until this afternoon which ones to use."

This was something of a surprise. The Terrans were expecting the Lyffans to develop rocket propulsion, the method that had first sent earthmen into space, and the Lyffan's problem of choice seemed as strange as if a cow were to have the problem of choosing whether to speak English or French.

When they reached the test site, the Terrans' surprise increased. They were expecting some kind of stationary test stand. Instead they found a small fleet, twenty-five complete ships, each somewhat larger than a Federation light cruiser. The test site looked like a field in which the ships had grown like corn.

"Each ship is equipped with a different propulsion method," Teeltl explained. "A few of them are, in essence, rockets, but we have concentrated more on the principles of attraction and repulsion. Ah, the first test has started."

One of the ships was moving slowly upward on a pillar of blue flame. "Actually," Teeltl continued, "rocket propulsion is the method we're least likely to use. Too inefficient, too cumbersome and too limited. It doesn't make sense to use most of your fuel merely to lift whatever fuel is left. But we wanted to give the system a trial. It may possess advantages we have not been able to predict. Ah, there goes another."

A second ship, this one with a red exhaust, was following the first. "We are also experimenting with different propellants, of course," Teeltl said mildly.

The Terrans were properly dumbfounded. "How long have you been working on space drives?" Pindar Smith asked.

"Four years," was the answer. "We got the idea when the People's Army started using rockets in battle. There were some earlier experiments with dynamite, but they were all inconclusive failures. All they taught us was that dynamite is an unsatisfactory fuel."

Three more rockets went up, each riding a stream of different colored fire. Then, after the control center reported that all five ships were in their calculated orbits, lunch was served.

The Terrans ate in silence. John Harlen especially felt glum. What he had witnessed so far was enough to qualify Lyff for membership in the Federation, and all he had seen were the rejects. The big show was yet to come.

What he felt was let down. His job was finished three years ahead of schedule, which would probably earn him a commendation. But he wasn't ready for his job to be finished yet. He still had three years' worth of plans to realize, plans that had suddenly become obsolete. He felt emptied.

He also felt vaguely guilty of cheating. The Lyffans had progressed in seven years farther than he'd planned to take them in ten, and it was almost all their own doing.

He'd really played only a minor role in the development of Lyff, and yet he and the rest of the Special Detail would most likely get the credit for the whole thing. John Harlen was not at all happy, and he was ashamed of himself for being unhappy.

The demonstration after lunch was terrifying.

"The front ship on the far right will be tested first," Gelph Gar-Pandyen Teeltl announced. "Please watch it very carefully."

They watched. If the ship could have been moved by intense stares, they would have moved it. Suddenly it vanished, and the air rushed in where it had been with the sound of thunder.

"Pretty," Teeltl murmured.

Ten more ships vanished in the same way, one right after the other, with a noise like a string of monstrous firecrackers.

"Interesting," John said, working hard to control his voice. "How did you do it?"

"It's really quite simple," the scientist responded. "As a matter of fact, we got the idea from the Guild of Metal Workers. Right after the war they developed, Mother knows how, a pressor-tractor beam device to help them handle the heavy plates required in spaceship construction. We're still not sure how the beam works, but we have a good idea what we can do with it. Some of the ships that just left simply clamped static tractor beams on distant stars. In this test some of them used Mother's Eye. They didn't move; Lyff moved out from under them. The others did much the same thing, but they pulled instead. Since the stars are too large to be moved, for all practical purposes, by these little ships, the ships moved toward the stars. It's really very simple."

"Yeah, simple," Ansgar said. "How fast can they go?"

"There is a theoretical limit of roughly one hundred eleven thousand, seven hundred and eighty sterbs per second, which is the speed at which the beam itself moves. Roughly the speed of light. However, there is a possibility

129

that we'll be able to multiply that velocity by itself. We don't know yet."

"What are *they* doing?" Smith shouted, pointing out toward the test site.

The remaining nine ships were floating lightly across the field. They danced and bounced with the air currents and the irregularities of the ground like silver bubbles. As they rose higher and higher in their effortless flight, they one by one winked out of sight.

"Pressor beams," Teeltl said proudly. "Strictly for interplanetary work. The ships rise to a safe height, and then clamp a tractor on whatever planet is most convenient. They— Oh look, here comes the first rocket. Isn't that a sight, though? Those rockets aren't much for traveling, but they're certainly spectacular to watch."

The ship descended easily, landing, as far as John could tell, on the very spot from which it had taken off. Behind it, like fireflies bright enough to be seen in daylight, came the other four rockets. The sound of their landing was an act of physical violence, but the landings themselves were accomplished with incredible ease.

The test was scheduled to last five days, long enough for the long-range pressor-tractor ships to complete their round trips, but John didn't stay for the rest of the show. He had another urgent message to send to Terra.

21

The last thing on Lyff John wanted to do that night was attend a joint session of the two houses of Parliament at the Temple, but he was under orders—not invitation, mind you, but orders—from the king to attend.

"Foolish waste of time," he muttered as he dressed in his finest clothes.

Ansgar Sorenstein and Pindar Smith, whose presence had also been commanded, agreed with John. "It's probably just some religious celebration or another," Smith said peevishly. "I don't see why we have to be there."

"We have to be there because King Osgard ordered us to," Sorenstein equally peevishly explained.

"All right," John said, "why did he give the order? In fact, why did he make an order out of it at all? The King has never done anything like this before."

"Mother knows," Ansgar replied. "I guess we'll find out when we get there."

The joint session was sitting in the main building of the Temple complex, a long, tall structure that looked like a streamlined Gothic cathedral. The Terrans arrived a few minutes before the session was scheduled to open, but the Mother's Guards at the door wouldn't let them in.

"What sort of nonsense is this?" Smith asked. "We were ordered to be here at this time. Why can't we go in?"

"I'm sure I don't know, sir," one of the guards answered. "When the High Priest gives us orders, he doesn't generally explain them."

"Great," John snapped. "Well, I, for one, am going back home."

"I'm sorry, sir," the guard said, "but I've been ordered to keep you here."

The Terrans fumed in silence for ten minutes. Then they were joined by General Garth.

"Hello there," he said. "Sorry I'm late. Testing, you know. I couldn't get away any earlier."

"That's okay," John said. "We didn't even know you were going to be here. Do you have any idea what this is all about?"

"No, I don't. All I know is that King Osgard ordered me to be here tonight."

"Orders seem to be a lot more common nowadays than they used to be," Ansgar commented.

"That's one of the disadvantages of a constitutional monarchy," John said. "Elected power takes itself a lot more seriously than hereditary power does."

Just then a brilliantly dressed acolyte came to the door and made a signal at the guards.

"Please come this way, gentlemen," one of the guards said. The three Terrans and the Lyffan general followed the guard into the Temple.

As they entered the door, a three-hundred voice chorus struck up the Lyffan national hymn.

Oh come, Mother's children,
Joyful, strong, and faithful,
Oh come, ye, Oh come, ye, to Mother's Knee;
Rest from your labors
In her place of comfort.
Oh come let us adore her,
Oh come let us adore her,
Oh come let us adore her: Mother dear.

The Temple was a fantasia of colors. Gauze banners in Mother's colors, saffron and purple, fell from the rafters halfway to the stone floor, at least fifty feet, and moved slowly back and forth in the vagrant air currents. Acolytes in gold and green lined the long aisle down which the

Terrans and the general marched in unconscious time to the music, and behind the acolytes, the full membership of both houses stood in respect and radiance. Scarlet, silver, vert, cadmium orange and amethyst struck at the Terrans' eyes like chromatic arrows.

And at the far end of the aisle, before a black and silver arras that hung from the ceiling to the floor, two men sat in plain wooden chairs. One was the High Priest, dressed in shining saffron robes, and the other was King Osgard, dressed in equally brilliant purple. As John, Ansgar, Pindar, and General Garth drew near, the king and the priest rose.

The High Priest extended his hands in benediction and the singing stopped. "M is for the men she has created," he intoned.

"O is for the orders she has given," the choir responded.

The responsory ran through five spellings of the word "Mother" and then fell off into silence.

Hurd, resplendent in scarlet and grey, stepped up beside the now thoroughly confused Terrans and said loudly, "In Mother's Hidden Name, so shall I speak."

"In Mother's Hidden Name, speak well, my son," the High Priest responded.

"By the authority Mother has given me through the people and the king, I wish to present four candidates for Mother's Undying Gratitude."

"Speak, my son, that we may know how these have earned Mother's Undying Gratitude."

Instead of Hurd, the choir responded, singing an elaborate anthem that told the story of Special Detail L-2, the Terran Federation, and the defeat of the Committee. When this was finished, the High Priest and King Osgard conferred for a moment, and then chanted in unison, "Let the candidates come forward."

The ceremony was a long and involved one, with many prayers from the High Priest and many anthems from the choir. Finally, however, King Osgard and the High Priest joined in decorating General Garth and each of the

Terrans with large gold medals hung on saffron and purple ribbons, Mother's Undying Gratitude; the choir performed a jubilant anthem; and, led by the king and the High Priest, everyone in the Temple marched solemnly outside.

"Congratulations!" Hurd said as soon as they were out of doors.

"Thanks," John answered, "but what was that all about? What does this medal mean?"

"Mother's Undying Gratitude? Why, John, that's the highest honor Lyff can bestow. You people are national heroes and official saints, that's what you are. Your birthdays will be holidays. Congratulations."

"Yeah, thanks." Something about all this was worrying John, and he couldn't figure out what it was.

"Have you heard the results of the tests yet?" someone asked the High Priest.

"Yes," he answered. "They came in just before the decoration ceremony began."

"So?"

"They're just about what we expected."

"That means we can go ahead, then."

"I think so."

"Hmm. Are you really happy about all this?"

"Of course I am. Why shouldn't I be?"

"I mean, don't you ever worry that this may not be the right thing to do? Don't you have any doubts about it at all?"

"Of course not. I know it's the right thing to do. Pardon me for quoting scripture, but 'And Mother looked upon her children, saying, "I wish somebody would make those kids behave." ' You're not going to argue with Garth Gar-Muyen Garth, are you?"

"No, that would be foolish. All right then, when do we begin?"

"We'd best wait until we've settled the problem of the invaders. It would never do to have them interrupt us in the middle of things, as it were."

22

"I've been a national hero and official saint for a week now, and I'm still not happy about it," John was talking with his new aide, Tchornyo Gar-Spolnyen Hiirlte.

"That I can't understand," Tchornyo said. "All Lyff is proud of you. Why should that make you unhappy?"

"If I knew that, I wouldn't be unhappy. Maybe I'd be happy, maybe I'd be angry, but I certainly wouldn't be sitting around worrying like this."

"Maybe you don't fully realize what Mother's Undying Gratitude means."

"Most likely I don't. Sometimes I wonder if I fully understand what anything means. Lyff is a very confusing planet."

"That medal means that you are one of Mother's chosen people. You have a place reserved for you in Mother's place of comfort. That's something any Lyffan would give up his life to have. You and the nine or ten others who have been awarded Mother's Undying Gratitude represent everything our religion means. Mothers tell their children to imitate you. Priests make sermons about you. This workshop will be a shrine. You should be very happy."

"How can I be one of Mother's chosen people if I don't believe in— Oh!"

"What's wrong?"

"I just realized why I'm unhappy. I didn't choose Mother, she chose me."

"That's right."

"Great. That means that whether I want to be or not, I'm still subject to Mother's Law."

"But you always were."

"Not in any way that showed. Not like this. But what bothers me most is that I don't know what Mother's Law is. Where did I put that copy of *The Book of Garth Gar-Muyen Garth?*"

"It's on your workbench. I'll get it for you."

John took twelve hours to read *The Book of Garth.* The archaic Lyffan in which it was written reduced his reading speed to less than half what it usually was.

As he read, he underlined certain passages. Some of these were passages he liked, such as, "Everything is possible. Sooner or later, everything must be. Not will be, must be. It is our duty to being alive to make as much of everything be as we possibly can, and everything is possible."

Another passage John underlined said, "Every act is either creative or destructive. There is nothing between.

"Every creative act is an act of love. Destruction is fear.

"Creating is continually spending the coin of your Self so that you will always have your Self to spend, and this is called Love.

"Destruction is a bankruptcy, when you don't have any of your Self to spend, and this is called being afraid.

"Everything that is not Love is fear."

But most of the passages John underlined were disturbing, even, in a sense, frightening. At the very least, they were proofs that he had lived on Lyff for seven years without even beginning to understand the planet or its people.

For instance, "It is of the nature of Love to expand, to embrace as much as possible, to clasp as much of everything as possible to the lover's bosom. Mother's love, being perfect, seeks always to embrace all creation, even those things that would deny her love." The implications of those two sentences were distressing.

"I've got to talk to the High Priest," John told Tchornyo. Then he left, taking his underlined copy of *The Book of Garth Gar-Muyen Garth* with him.

"Of course, my son," the High Priest said. "I am always glad to be able to explain scriptural difficulties, and especially to one who has earned Mother's Undying Gratitude."

"Thank you, Father," John said, opening *The Book of Garth*. "I've marked the places that gave me trouble. Here's one."

"Ah yes," the High Priest said, glancing at the passage to which the book had opened. "The expansiveness of perfect love. But why should it trouble you? The meaning is perfectly clear."

"The meaning is clear enough, Father. What bothers me are the implications."

"Indeed?"

"Yes. The implication is that Mother's love is a conquering thing; that is, that Mother is likely to love by force those who do not love her by choice."

"That's true."

"And when we consider this passage, 'And Mother looked upon her children, saying, 'I wish someone would make those kids behave,' the implications become strong enough to justify a crusade, a sort of religious imperialism."

"My son, have you ever thought of becoming a theologian?"

"No, Father, I haven't."

"What a pity. Mother seems to have given you a great native talent for theology. It seems a shame to let it go to waste."

John went home a few hours later with all of his fears fully realized.

"Mother's hair," someone said in surprise as the High Priest entered the room. "What are you doing here at this time of day?"

"I've just been talking to John Gar-Terrayen Harlen."

"Oh yes, John. Clever, isn't he."

"Much too clever. I gave him a copy of *The Book of Garth* a few weeks ago, and now he's reasoned out our whole plan."

"He knows what we're going to do?"

"Yes, but he doesn't know that he knows it. He was bothered by the implications of certain passages, but that's all."

"Then he *doesn't* know what we're going to do."

"No, but he knows why we're going to do it, which is nearly as bad. We'll have to keep our eyes on these Terrans. They could become dangerous."

"Now the knight moves in right angles, two spaces in one direction and one space in another. Do you understand that?" Ansgar Sorenstein was trying to each Tchornyo how to play chess.

"But *why* does it move so oddly?" Tchornyo was not the most apt student Ansgar could have found.

"Mother's nose! How should I know why? It just does, that's all."

"As a teacher," John interrupted, "brother Ansgar here makes a splendid dalber-watcher."

"Oh no," Tchornyo said. "The trouble is that I'm so slow."

This conversation could have gone on for hours, but Pindar Smith ran noisily into the room with a message that put a temporary end to chess.

"It's from General Garth," he shouted excitedly.

"Hurrah for General Garth," Ansgar jeered. "What does he have to say?"

"The message says, 'Radar reports fleet approaching Lyff.' "

"Good Lord," John said, "they're here already. Three years early."

As they dashed out of the room, Ansgar said, "This only goes to prove the old proverb."

"Which one?" John asked.

"You know, 'If anything can possibly go wrong, it will.' "

"You, sir, are a dalberson clown." They got into their cars and drove off at top speed for the testing field.

23

Admiral Bellman was enjoying his tea in unusual peace when his yeoman ran into the office. "Message from Lyff," the yeoman said.

"Oh God! Why is it that every crisis on that damned planet comes to my attention at tea time, Harry? You'd think it happened on purpose."

"Yes, sir," the yeoman said. He put the message on Bellman's desk and returned to the outer office.

The admiral ignored the message until he'd finished his tea. "It takes twenty-five days for a message to reach here from Lyff," he explained to himself. "Whatever it is, it can wait until I've finished my tea."

When he'd read the message, Admiral Bellman said, "My God, it's too late. They left a week ago."

Then he sat for a long time in silence.

The message said, "Revise all estimates of time required for Lyffan project. Fleet of at least twenty-five ships already in existence. Advise all concerned to approach Lyff with extreme caution. Send diplomats to arrange admission to Federation. Harlen."

24

"We're entering the Lyffan system now, sir," the navigator said in a voice the intercom stripped of all tone and emotion.

"Thank you," Captain Bayle said. He flicked a switch and the intercom's humming died.

Though he didn't look it, Captain Bayle was a very worried man. This was his first major command, this convoy of two hundred ships, and he knew from the bottom of his pessimistic heart that something was going to go wrong. The convoy's mission was a fairly simple one to be sure, escorting and protecting two troopships full of scientists, but no Federation fleet of comparable size had ever come so close to enemy territory before, and anything could happen. The closeness to enemy territory was emphasized by the fact that the sole purpose of the expedition was to study a captured enemy ship. Captain Bayle had plenty to worry about.

The intercom made a noise like a horsefly. Damn! Why couldn't people just leave him alone for a while? Why couldn't they let him worry in peace? He flicked the intercom switch again and snapped, "Bayle here. What is it?"

"Warrant Officer Ritch Haln, sir, distant identification room." The only difference between this tinny voice and the navigator's was that this one tended to drone.

"Yes, Haln. What do you want?" That the intercom no doubt translated his own voice into the kind of tinny abstraction that so irritated him did not contribute to Captain Bayle's tranquillity.

"D-I screen report, sir. Three, four hundred ships at extreme range."

Automatically, even as he spoke, Bayle pressed a button marked "All Ships—General Quarters." Ignoring the sudden clangor of bells, he asked, "Whose are they? Do you recognize them?"

"No sir. I've never seen anything like them before." Haln was along on this trip mainly because of his experience seven years before aboard the *Terran Beaver*. If he had been able to identify the approaching fleet as enemy ships, there'd be no problem, only a battle, which was something Captain Bayle felt sure he could handle. But with the identity of the fleet left in doubt like this, there was nothing but problem. They could still be enemy ships; that they were unfamiliar to Haln didn't mean very much, because his experience consisted of one encounter with only one enemy ship. But they could be friendly, too; they could belong to some previously unknown race. The possibilities were endless.

"Captain Bayle? Are you still there?"

"Oh, I'm sorry, Haln. I was thinking. Ah . . . What's their velocity, Haln?"

"Point oh one three c and steady . . . No, they're beginning to accelerate."

"That means they've spotted us. Propulsion?"

"Ah . . . They don't seem to have any, sir."

"Nonsense, man. They *have* to have some means of propulsion."

"Yes sir. But it doesn't register on the screens, sir."

"Something new, I suppose. Hmm. Thank you, Mister Haln. Over and out." Captain Bayle flicked the switch once more and hurried, full of worry, to the bridge.

The two fleets met an hour later. The Federation ships were drawn up in campaniliform battle order, with all defense systems fully activated and all offensive systems warmed up and ready. The other fleet had assumed an arrangement that defied mathematical analysis, much to Captain Bayle's deepened distress.

Neither side seemed willing to fire the first shot, though the Federation defense system was designed to make the second shot, if needed, a thoroughly crushing one. However, the strange fleet seemed to be unwilling to respond to any of the standard identification signals, which was a bad sign.

There was a much worse sign, though. The strange fleet was moving backward now at exactly the speed with which the Federation fleet was moving forward. This was a bad sign because it was impossible, and the impossible is always ominous.

"Sir, would you look at this for a minute?" The young radarman looked as confused as Captain Bayle felt.

Bayle stepped over to the radar sphere and looked into it. Then he blinked once or twice, shook himself, and said in a low voice, "Well I'll be perpetually damned."

The alien ships were arranged in a formation that spelled out the words, "Welcome to Lyff."

25

"... Of course, the moment we saw the radar screen we knew you were Feds, so we decided to give you a little surprise." It was twelve hours later and, in Lyffdarg, John Harlen was explaining things to Captain Bayle.

"A few more little surprises like that and I'm dead. Practical jokes involving three hundred spaceships are just too much for me. And where did those ships come from, anyhow? I thought this was an undeveloped planet."

"It was, but the Lyffans learn fast. They built that fleet from scratch in three years."

"Amazing."

"You don't know the half of it. We didn't know they had such a fleet until this morning. They managed to build it without our noticing."

"Why the secrecy?"

"There wasn't any secrecy. We simply didn't notice what they were doing. We expected them to go through the usual process from primitive rockets to more sophisticated models and finally to actual spaceships, and that process was what we were looking for. We didn't expect them to bypass the whole developmental stage, and so we didn't notice them doing it."

"Very confusing."

"Isn't it just? I'm glad the Lyffans are on our side."

Hurd Gar-Olnyn Saarlip was suffering a confusion of loyalties. Soon, he knew, Lyff would be invited to join the Terran Federation. As prime minister, he would no doubt be the principal Lyffan negotiator, and the future of his home planet would be in his hands. It would be [...] job to see to it that the negotiations favored Lyff.

But he was also a citizen of the Federation. He remembered very clearly taking the oath seven years ago. If it weren't for the Federation, he'd still be a common criminal, and maybe an executed one at that. He owed everything to the Federation, even his present office.

If during the negotiations some point should arise on which Lyff and the Federation differed, to which side should he be loyal? If he had to betray the interests of one side or the other, which side should he betray? Or was there maybe some way to avoid the conflict altogether?

No matter how hard he thought about it, Hurd could find no solution for this problem. Finally he gave up and asked the High Priest what to do.

The High Priest told him exactly what to do.

26

For a month the Federation fleet loafed on the ground while the Federation scientists studied the Migrant ship. Some of the officers were pressed into service as teachers, training the Lyffans in the complex art of space warfare, but the enlisted men were free to roam at will through Lyffdarg and its neighboring communities.

The city's red-light district enjoyed an economic boom unprecedented in the history of the planet, and the little sisters grew wealthy enough to form, at last, their own guild, the Guild of Entertainers. Mother Balnya, for example, quickly became the richest woman on Lyff, prompting a parliamentary investigation of vice in Lyffdarg that dissolved in laughter when she revealed, in an exclusive Lyffdarg *Chronicle* interview, that she had carefully bribed all the investigators.

The Lyffan fleet was officially declared to be the Royal Lyffan Space Navy as soon as King Osgard, General Garth, Captain Bayle, and John Harlen were satisfied that it could hold its own in any interplanetary battle, and General Garth became Admiral Garth.

The Feds were especially interested in the unorthodox drive and weapon systems the RLSN had developed. "In many ways," Captain Bayle said, "these chaps are far ahead of us. I wouldn't be a bit surprised if they were to come up with an original faster-than-light drive tomorrow. In fact, I wouldn't be a bit surprised to learn that they already had an ftl drive and were using it for something else. It's a good thing they're on our side."

It was a month of idylls, broken only by the usual

frictions that are bound to arise when large numbers of healthy young men are turned loose in a new and alien environment. A few spacers, drunk on Lyffan wine, accidentally defiled the Temple; others got in trouble by mistaking respectable women for little sisters; a few brawls occurred, and many more smaller fights, but in general the Lyffans and the Feds were quite pleased with each other.

Toward the end of the month a courier arrived from Terra bearing the credentials and other documents necessary to constitute John Harlen Federation Ambassador to Lyff.

"How can I be an ambassador, Doc? I don't know anything about diplomacy."

"You're a national hero," Doctor Jellfte explained. "You don't need diplomacy. Diplomacy is only a stopgap, a substitute for mutal trust. You and the Lyffans don't need a substitute. It would be an insult to send a diplomat to Lyff."

"There are flaws in your argument."

"There usually are. So what? You're still a better choice for Ambassador to Lyff than any professional diplomat would be. I don't care if my explanations are wrong as long as the fact remains unchanged."

Ambassador Harlen's first official act, after presenting his credentials, was to invite Lyff to join the Federation. King Osgard responded with a few words about trade agreements, mutual defense pacts, cultural exchanges and other interplanetary amenities. Ambassador Harlen's second official act was to schedule a series of high-level meetings to discuss such matters as trade agreements *et cetera*.

This month of peace ended abruptly with the arrival in force of the Migrant invaders.

27

The enemy fleet was three days away when Lyffan radar discovered it.

"There must be at least a thousand ships in that fleet," Admiral Garth told Captain Bayle. "They look like flies around a dalber's head."

"A thousand of them and five hundred of us," Bayle said. "Considering that we have three days' notice, we're pretty evenly matched."

The enemy fleet did indeed look like flies around a dalber's head. From the Feds' viewpoint, the invading fleet looked like a swarm of mayflies, but the total effect of great numbers concentrated in a relatively small area was the same. At any rate, the invaders formed, on that first day, a very nearly perfect target.

The Lyffans struck the first blow. Using long-range pressor beams, they studded the area directly ahead of the invaders with mines and thermonuclear devices provided by the Federation fleet.

Thousands of Lyffans watched this first blow through telescopes, and with each explosion a cheer went up that could be heard all over the planet. When, after a dozen or so such explosions, the invaders changed formation, expanding to occupy a much larger and less immediately vulnerable volume, a groan was heard on Lyff as loud as the previous cheers.

Meanwhile, the RLSN and the Federation fleet took up positions behind the Lyffan system's outer planets. "In the game of war," John Harlen explained to anyone who would listen, "the strongest move is an offensive move, but the strongest position is a defensive one. The important things are surprise, advantage of ground, and attack from several quarters, and we have all three working for us. All the enemy has is superior forces, and it only requires a few well-planned surprises to change that."

War *is* a game, in the same way that chess is. As in chess, the players generally alternate moves. The only way the effect of the first move can be judged with any accuracy is by observing the opponent's countermove. The second move, made by the invaders, was to send a rain of missiles down on Lyff.

Very few of these missiles got past the Lyffan defenses. Most of them were destroyed harmlessly in space by objects—stones, logs, scrap metal, anything with enough mass to do the job—sent against them via pressor beams. Others were deflected by pressor beams and sent back on the invading fleet. Of the few that did get through, only one or two actually did any serious damage. Lyff was sparsely populated, and even if all the enemy missiles had landed on the planet, most of them would have landed in unpopulated areas. The only direct hit was scored against Spolnyendarg, a small agricultural center at the foot of the Northern Mountains. The town was completely destroyed, of course, and all of its fifteen hundred residents were killed, but the enemy's losses were far greater than Lyff's, and its resources were far less.

Although the bombardment continued through the second day of the battle, the predominant mood on Lyff was highly optimistic. "We'll blow the Mother-lorn dalbersons out of the Mother-lorn sky," accurately expressed the popular opinion.

The mood of Lyff's defenders, on the other hand, darkened slowly through the second day. It quickly became obvious that the original estimates of the enemy's strength were far short of the reality. Instead of a thousand ships, the invaders seemed to have more like two thousand ships. This became so obvious as the fleet neared Lyff that by midday John Harlen gave up explaining the art war and took to saying encouraging but meaningless ogans. That neither Lyffan mines nor their own de-lected missiles caused the enemy ships to swerve from their Lyffward course was regarded as being exceedingly ominous.

The enemy's vanguard entered the Lyffan system early on the third day. It consisted of some three hundred scout ships much like the one destroyed seven years before by the *Terran Beaver* and the one captured by the People's Army just before the fall of the Committee.

The scouts crossed the orbit of Big Sister, the outermost planet, without incident and apparently without noticing that there were a hundred light cruisers hiding behind Big Sister.

The next planet in toward Mother's Eye was Little Sis-ter, a useless chunk of rock on which were hidden fifty Federation destroyers. Little Sister was directly in the scouts' path, but instead of changing course, the scouts destroyed the planet, peppering it with bombs until there was nothing left of Little Sister and the fifty destroyers but an insubstantial cloud of dissociated ions through which the enemy passed easily.

"My God!" Captain Bayle screamed. "Those destroyers were twenty-five percent of my fleet."

Admiral Garth was grave. "Why did they destroy Little Sister?" he asked. "Why didn't they just go around her? What kind of people *are* they?"

The scouts moved on, passing the orbits of four more planets, destroying everything that got in their way, but not turning aside to destroy anything that was not in their way, not reducing their speed, not doing anything the defenders expected them to do. And behind them came the main enemy fleet.

Finally, just as the main fleet entered the system, the scouts crossed the orbit of Poor Sister and all hell broke loose. Lyffan pressor-tractor installations hastily estab-lished on Poor Sister spread chaos through the scouts, dis-rupting battle formation and causing collisions.

Forty Lyffan ships armed with entropy devices attack the enemy scouts from the rear, converting the scout drive energy to inert lead and rendering the squadron powerless and helpless. Federation missiles completed the carnage, and for three hours the planet Lyff gloried in the light of two suns, Mother's Eye and the dying scouts.

Unfazed by this, the main body of the Migrant fleet poured past Big Sister without changing speed or course.

As the size of not only the enemy fleet but especially the ships that comprised it became evident, the defenders' worries deepened toward despair. "My God, look at those monsters," Captain Bayle said. "And there are almost two thousand of them."

A typical enemy ship—the scouts were not at all typical—was roughly a mile and a half long, with other proportions to match. Each ship was studded with angular projections that were obviously weapon housings. In the whole fleet, aside from escort and scout ships, there was not a sign of streamlining in any form.

"One thing's sure," John Harlen said. "Those ships weren't designed to land anywhere. Any kind of atmosphere would tear them apart, and most likely they can't take gravity either. I wonder . . ." Full of a beautiful idea, John rushed off to the Lyffan home defense center.

"Sure we can do it," the home defense chief told him, "but I don't see what good it'll do."

"It can't do any harm, can it?"

"No, I don't think so."

"Then try it. It's as likely to work as anything else."

The Federation-RLSN battle plan, calling for an attack on the invaders from the rear after they passed Big Sister, had to be abandoned when it became clear that by the time the last enemy ships passed Big Sister, the first ones would be attacking Lyff.

"We can't win," Captain Bayle mourned. "There are too many of them. They're too big. They— Oh, what's the use? We can't possibly win."

"You're probably right," Admiral Garth replied. "But

n if we can't win, we can at least lose gloriously. I
y attack now and Mother blast the battle plan."

The defending fleets swarmed out from their hiding
places, all weapons blazing like newborn stars. The
enemy, still not bothering to change course or reduce
speed, responded with a barrage that seemed to turn that
volume of space into solid death and destruction. In the
first ten minutes of the battle, at least a hundred ships
were lost on each side.

"At this rate, they can destroy us in another thirty
minutes," Bayle said, "and it will take us three hours to
destroy— What the hell is Lyff doing?"

Lyff was putting John Harlen's idea into operation.
Every pressor beam on the planet was sending up a
steady stream of metal cylinders, all of which exploded
long before they reached the enemy fleet.

"Last ditch defense," Admiral Garth said with sad
pride. "Lyff will die fighting or not at all." He sniffed,
blushed, and went on, "Mother can be proud of her
children today. The Lyffan people will— Look at that!"

The enemy ships were one by one dissolving in clouds
of bright yellow flame.

"We don't have anything that will do that," Bayle
shouted excitedly.

"Neither do we," shouted Garth.

The enemy ships ploughed on. Each one, as it reached
the orbit of Poor Sister, burst into flames, and still the
fleet ploughed on. Garth and Bayle called off the defending ships, and still the enemy burned. For eight hours,
while the defenders stood off and watched, the huge Migrant ships bore into that curtain of brilliant yellow fire
from which none of them emerged.

"It's a miracle," Bayle whispered.

"Yellow is Mother's color," Admiral Garth said simply.

28

"It was really very simple," John explained next day. "As soon as I realized that the big ships were never meant to enter an atmosphere, I remembered what happened to the ship we captured when an atmosphere entered it. Those cylinders we sent up were full of compressed air, that's all. We taped grenades to the cylinders, and when the grenades went off, the cylinders released a cloud of pure Lyffan air. And when the ships entered that cloud, they oxidized. Simple."

"But you had no proof it would work," Bayle said.

"No, but I had no proof it wouldn't work, either, and since we were losing anyhow, it made sense to try."

"Now?" somebody asked the High Priest.

"Why not? It's the perfect time."

"Right after the battle?"

"Indeed. It's as though Mother herself were promising success."

The victory celebration lasted five days and nights. There were elaborate religious ceremonies and processions, spectacular demonstrations of skill by the victorious navies, gala concerts of ancient and modern music, and enormous feasts at which everybody got drunk. There was continual dancing in the streets. There was laughter and rejoicing everywhere.

The climax of the celebration was a monster party for the Federation spacemen on the evening of the fifth day. This party, given in the Temple amphitheater, was at-led by everyone who could possibly attend. A handful spacemen had to stand sentry duty, but the rest of the Federation crewmen flocked into the great amphitheater.

"You know what this reminds me of?" asked Pindar Smith, gesturing at the little sisters who were dancing between the tables.

Doctor Jellfte finished the kabnon leg he was munching on and said, "I'll bite. What does this remind you of?"

"A Roman orgy, that's what."

"No," John broke in. "Lyff is too puritanical for that. Look at all the priests and acolytes in the balconies. Mother wouldn't approve of a Roman orgy, and they're here to see to it that a Roman orgy doesn't happen."

There was a sudden disturbance. A man shouted hoarsely, a girl screamed.

"There's someone else who thinks this is like a Roman orgy," Ansgar said.

"He's too drunk to think much of anything," John contradicted.

"He seems to think a lot of that dancing girl," Smith said.

"And here come the priests." John's voice was boozily triumphant. "Orgies simply don't happen on Lyff. Mother doesn't like them."

The party threatened to be endless. The feast alone went on and on for three hours, with speeches and entertainment between the courses. And after the feast the serious drinking and speech-making started. Everyone made a speech who wanted to, and several who didn't want to—Captain Bayle and John Harlen, for example— were coerced into speaking. Even the drunken sailor who'd tried whatever it was he'd tried with the dancing girl made a speech.

"As you know," Bayle's speech began, "this is both a victory celebration and a farewell party. Tomorrow afternoon we leave for Terra." Loud groans. "Our mission is accomplished and more than accomplished. We came to examine one enemy ship and stayed to destroy the entire fleet. Now it's time to go home again."

The last speech was made by the Prime Minister of Lyff, Hurd Gar-Olnyn Saarlip. It was the shortest speech of the evening.

"I wish to call to your attention," he said, "the fact that the balconies are now occupied by the First and Second Embraces of Mother's Guards, and that the gates are held by the Third and Fourth Embraces. By order of King Osgard Gar-Osgardnyen Osgard and in Mother's Hidden Name I arrest you. You will not be ill-treated, but all resistance will be crushed without mercy."

Then, avoiding John Harlen's eyes, Hurd left the amphitheater.

The sentries guarding the Federation fleet were not in a good humor. The lights from the amphitheater could be seen from the hill outside of the town that the fleet was on; and every once in a while a particularly nasty gust of wind would carry sounds of the revelry. The sergeant of the guard was in a particularly vile humor. "Why," he asked the officer of the guard, a young second lieutenant of marines, "don't they at least relieve us after a six-hour watch so at least my boys can get in on the end of the party at least?"

The lieutenant shrugged. "Let's face it sergeant, after six hours of a blast like the one that's going on in there," he indicated the amphitheater, "there isn't going to be anyone left in any condition to guard anything."

"And that's another thing," the sergeant said. "What the hell are we guarding these damn ships against anyway?"

"Look," the lieutenant was getting aggravated, "we guard these ships on Terra, we guard these ships on Luna Base, so there is no reason why we shouldn't guard these ships on Lyff."

Just then there was a knock on the door of the guard shack. When the sergeant opened the door a group of lite sisters walked in. "We were sent over by Prime Minister Hurd," one of the sisters started, "to see if you boys wanted company," another of the girls finished breathlessly.

It would have been noted, if there had been anyone noting such things, that as each one of the guards completed his circuit of the Federation fleet and went into the guard shack for his ten-minute break, he didn't come out again. It would also have been noted that the noises emanating from the shack gradually increased in volume and gaiety. It would have eventually been noted that there were no guards patrolling the ships any more, that they were all inside the guard shack.

As a matter of fact, it *was* noted. Ten minutes after the last guard entered the shack there came another knock on the door. When it was opened, a man in the uniform of a major in Mother's Guards came in. "This building is surrounded by an Embrace of Mother's Guards," he said. "By order of King Osgard Gar-Osgardnyen Osgard and in Mother's Hidden Name you are all under arrest. In the Name of Mother I ask you not to cause any trouble, we don't want to hurt any of you."

"It's all my fault," John mourned. The amphitheater was dark now, empty of all gaiety and full only of disgruntled men.

"How could you have known?" Ansgar Sorenstein was doing his best to cheer John Harlen, but with little success.

"I *did* know. That's what bothers me so much. It's all in *The Book of Garth Gar-Muyen Garth*. I knew it all the time, and I didn't do anything about it."

"What the hell are you talking about?"

"Mother, that's what I'm talking about. She wants to gather all her children together. She wants someone to make them behave. Lyff's religion is evangelical, and we've just contributed to the first interstellar crusade.

And I knew it all the time and just didn't realize wh[...]
I knew. Damn!"

John Harlen refused to be consoled.

Before the fleet took off, the High Priest personally
blessed each ship and King Osgard delivered an exhorta-
tion.

"All Lyff admires you," he said. "Indeed, all Lyff en-
vies you. None of us who must stay at home would not
give up everything he owns for the privilege of joining
you in your glorious task of spreading Mother's Word
among her unheeding children. But it is Mother's Will
that we remain behind, our task accomplished, while you
go forth to convert the heathen and reclaim the Place of
Comfort. Go then, knowing that all Lyff is praying for
you."

Then the Temple Choir sang the national hymn. The
last verse was drowned in the noise of a million thunder-
storms and the ships were gone.

"You know," King Osgard said, "I never really thought
this would happen."

"You did quite well, then," the High Priest replied.

"Actually, it was all your doing. I never would have
thought of fomenting a rebellion against myself. If it had
been up to me, I'd have gotten rid of the nobility by
waging war on *them,* not on myself. Mother should be
very happy with you."

The High Priest smiled.

29

"Message from Lyff, sir," the yeoman said.

"From Lyff? Impossible. I'm not having tea. Messages from Lyff only arrive at tea time. You should know that by now."

"Sir?"

"I'm just joking, Harry. It's been a long, hard day, and if I don't make jokes I'm likely to make threats, and I don't have anyone to threaten, so— Oh, never mind. Give me the message. I'll study it on the way home."

He stuffed the message into his pocket and promptly forgot about it. Later that night, when he was getting ready for bed, he remembered the message, extracted it from his pocket, and read it.

"What the hell is *this* all about?" he exploded.

The message said, "Be good, children. Mother is coming to get you."

"Is something wrong, dear?" Mrs. Bellman asked.

"No, it's nothing. Just somebody's stupid idea of a practical joke."

When he awoke next morning, the sky was full of ships.

Are you missing out on some great Jove/HBJ books?

"You can have any title in print at Jove/HBJ delivered right to your door! To receive your Jove/HBJ Shop-At-Home Catalog, send us 25¢ together with the label below showing your name and address.

JOVE PUBLICATIONS, INC.
Harcourt Brace Jovanovich, Inc.
Dept. M.O., 757 Third Avenue, New York, N.Y. 10017

NAME_____

ADDRESS_____

CITY_____STATE_____

NT-1   ZIP_____